What's Done In The Dark
By
Allysha Hamber

Acknowledgements

Well…it's that time again. You know the one thing I've noticed in writing the acknowledgement section for each different book that I write? It is the fact that very few names remain the same. The rest have faded out of your life, for some reason or another. Not that it matters, because God is always faithful and just to replace them with new ones.

So, with that said, to those who are no longer here for whatever reason it may be, I thank you anyway because somewhere along the road in my life, you meant something to me, so it's all good.

To all the media and radio stations, along with all the bookstores and flea markets, I thank you for all the pushing and promotion of my books.

Special Thanks To…

Those who stood by me (The one's who been real), believed in me and **actually** *wanted to see to fly, even when the rough winds of the storms, threatened to ground my dreams.*

My blood…My sisters, Punkin (The Big Gurl!), Lynne and Rhonda. My brothers…Big Slug, Wayne, Q, Fabian, Ron Macon, Fred and Mont. My Neices and nephews, my blood: (Taderra, Quionna, Miracle, Chris & Cory, CJ) My God Nieces and Nephews: Jayla, MaRisha, Romia, Aerionna, Puff, Ashley, Cee-Cee, Pinky, Dominque and my baby girl India) Ya'll know I love the kids!

To my family bound to me by love and not by blood…here we go…My Uncle Wolf A.K.A Unc (Holdin' it down on Mimika!) Larry A.K. A. Law (Stay exactly the way you are, always puttin' a smile on my face, even when I don't want too), Poppy, BrokeNeck, Vincel, Uncle Daryl and Uncle Floyd. Ruth, Lana, Tonya, Dee, The Bishop Don Won and the Jump Off Lounge Family, Momma Whitby, Jean and the Whitby Family. My co-workers @ Nu-Way Trucking, Virgil (Poppa Smurf), Ray, Lanell, Zoe, Crockett, Dave, Nova, Ed, Tunisia (One of my biggest fans), Beverly , Tony and *Kellie. Mary Wilson (Thank you for all your love and support, may God continue to shine down upon you and all you do!).*

And Now Introducing…

Weather it's through thug love, or hood love. I would like to give special shouts outs to the following people because beyond the joys and pains, we've all hung in there, together.

My girls…I hate to even start listing names cause for real, you know if you been true to the game or not! It seems like every time I get ready to show love, somebody always have to fuck up the party! But shouts out anywayz to Tanya A.K.A TMA, Cennetta and Dana. Ms. Kim, the only real homegirl holdin' it down on the 59' block (thanks for the supportin' the books). Sandra Mattox, holdin' it down in Columbus, Baby Momma in Detroit (Hollywood), Simone Lowe and the rest of my girls in various FPC's and FCI's (Keep Ya Head UP! What God has for you is for you and the system can't take it away, ya heard me! I Miss you guys!)

To all ya'll who thrive off that drama, it's almost '09 and I'm no longer on yo' dime! I got money to make! If you didn't see yo' name here, don't hate on me, hate the bullshi*t you bring to the table!

My boyz…My hood nigga's… Jay (the coolest n-i-g-g-a on the block. Keep That Swagga! Much love to you, Always!) Uncle Kenny (Thanks for all the listening and I thank you for all the encouragement you've given me in pursuing my dreams.) Frankie & Suge(ya'll good people, stay that way!) Kay-Kay, Toi, Lil Curtis, Hank & Tee-Tee.

*Last but certainly not least… my best friend, my homie, my heart, my everything…words can not express what you've been to me. I have always searched for that special kind of love in my life and I am sooooooo blessed to have found it in you. The love I have for you keeps me safe and comforted in my weakest hours. It brings me strength when I can't find it on my own. It makes me smile when I'm down and the best part is…it's unconditional! Ya'll want a name? It's not necessary…for those of you who really know **God**, should feel the same way as I do!*

3

Dedication

This book, as with every positive thing I do in life, is for my babies…My Princes', Dorian Jones and Davion Hamber along with my princess Tamara Hamber. My heart will always, always belong to you! Momma loves you very, very much! Nothing or no one, has the power to <u>ever</u> change that!

Also: To My mother, Ozella Jones Foster… No matter where I go in life, know that things haven't always been good between us but I carry you in my heart, close to me, Always!

What's Done In The Dark

"… *Girl you know that I'm committed, to someone else. So why you wanna push me to the limit? Everytime I come near you, I wanna do what you want me to do but it wouldn't be cool.*

I'm not cold, so why am I shaking girl? You put me through some serious changes and my mind, keeps tellin' me to turn and wallk away… oh girl I'd better go, before it to late…

You know I want to kiss you but I better leave now. I want to stay here all night but I need to go. You make me weak, so while I'm strong… I'd better leave well enough, alone…"

Chapter One...Terri

"...It's mornin' and we've slept the night away. It happened, now we can't turn back the hands of time..."

Ding Dong...ding dong.

Oh hell no, that is not my damn door bell ring. What crazy idiot would be at my door at...?

I rubbed my eyes and glanced at the tiny red numbers on the black clock on the night stand.

Two AM? Who the hell?

Whoever it was, was in for two things. First of all, I was gonna cuss they ass out for ringing my damn door bell like they the damn FBI. Secondly, beat'em down if they woke up my son AJ. It took me two hours to get him down to sleep because he hadn't been feeling well. He was just getting over both an ear infection and a cold.

I rolled over and closed my eyes, hoping it all was just a dream.

Ding dong.

No such luck. I flipped my black silk comforter over to the other side of the bed. It still smelled strongly of Arman's Safari Cologne from earlier that day.

Ummmm, the aroma began to awaken my senses. He'd make good love to me on the living room floor as we watched **Jayson** stroke the hell out of **Lyric** on top of a cash register. As good as Jayson was though, he had nothing on Arman'.

7

I closed my eyes and revisited the moment...*ummmm*. He was, as always, the perfect lover. Attentive, passionate, un-demanding and freaky... oh so freaky. I reminisced about the way he slid his tongue between my thighs and made passionate figure eights around my clit. The way he slowly spread my butt cheeks apart, wet it with his tongue and softly blew inside my love tunnel.

He blew, he licked and he fingered me to heights unknown. I reflected upon the way he mounted me on top of his lap and pounded inside my walls with a motion so perfectly structured and pleasure that I felt so deep.

My hand slid between my thighs and I squeezed there tightly in his memory. Oh... I missed him so much... his stroke, his smell, the taste of his sweat, his heartbeat... his... *ding dong...*

FUCK!

I rolled off the bed, grabbed my golden silk robe from behind the door and headed down the small hallway. I stopped along the way to peak in on AJ and make sure this fool, whoever it was, hadn't awakened him. I glanced inside and thankfully, he was still soundly asleep.

I clicked on the living room light and I paused mid-step, thinking it could be Arman' at the door. Maybe he'd forgotten his door key, as he so often did, having to hide it from his wife Alicia all the time. Maybe he'd settled things at the hospital and decided to stop back by and spend the night with us. He's been heavily stressed from his wife's early labor and their new baby girl being born sick with a blood disease. I'm sure he needed to unwind and relax. And I certainly didn't mind that it was me he chose to do it with.

I was always glad to have my man home with me. Yeah, he was married on paper but in his heart, I knew he belonged to me. I truly believed that and though I'd never let on or stress him about it, it pissed me off to see him go home to a woman every night that didn't deserve him. She couldn't love him like I could, that, I was sure of.

It ate me up inside, wondering... wondering if he made love to her like he made love to me. If she'd screamed out his name in the same operic range as I had, only hours before. The thought alone was turning my stomach.

In any event, I rushed to the bathroom to check my eyes for crust, my mouth for any signs of dried up drool and I wet my fingers and ran them through my hair. I popped the cap on the Colgate and put a dab of toothpaste in my mouth, swished it around with my tongue and proceeded on my way to the living room.

I unlatched the double bolted locks and pulled back the door with the chain still attached. If it was Arman' and I didn't do that, I'd never hear the end of it.

Through the six inch crack, I could see Pooh, Arman's sister sitting on the top step with her head down inside of her

9

hands. She was crying hysterically. I immediately unlatched the chain, pulled opened the door and proceeded outside to see what was wrong.

"Pooh, are you okay sweetie?"

She slowly lifted her head and turned to me. When I saw her face, I knew something was terribly wrong.

My first mind told me it was Cory, Arman's best friend and her "on again, off again" boyfriend. After her ex-boyfriend Kevin got another woman pregnant while they were still in a relationship together, for the life of me, I couldn't understand why she would want to date Cory. Kevin was a dog, true but Cory was an international hoe! Complete with skanks in damn near every area code. Eventually, I knew he was bound to hurt Pooh.

Pooh was a twenty-six-year-old sister struggling to be an up and coming attorney. Her only downfall was that she thought she had to have a thug as her bed mate. Don't get me wrong, every woman wants a man with a little bit of thug in him, but sometimes, you have to recognize when the brother is just trifling, like Cory.

I'd seen her upset before after one of their little lover's spats but this was something different. I could see it in her eyes. This was something very, very serious.

I stepped onto the porch as Pooh slowly rose to her feet. She stumbled as she tried to climb the last step and reached for the metal porch rail to catch her balance. I rushed over to grab her by the arm.

"Pooh, what's wrong? What is it? What happened? Tell me what's wrong."

"It's...its Arman'...you gotta go inside with me... he... please, take me inside so I can sit down. My head is spinning outta control."

I braced my arm around her waist and helped her through the door. The weight of her body felt like a ton of lead as I practically dragged her across the thick carpet. I helped her down onto the crème colored leather sofa.

"Let me get you something to drink," I said, placing her purse and keys down on the mirrored end table beside her.

"No, no I'm fine. Please," she said, patting the seat beside her. "I need to tell you this before I lose what little strength I have left."

"Okay, just let me get you a towel or..."

"Terri! Please! Sit down!" she yelled.

I jumped at the intensity of her voice.

What the hell?

I took a seat beside her. She was a nervous wreck and I was becoming more frightened by the minute. She grabbed my hand inside of hers and looked into my eyes. There was so much sadness there. Her mocha blend of eye shadow and foundation were stained from the previous tears she'd shed.

She was a smaller version of her brother, with the same light Carmel complexion and the same almond shaped eyes. Her lashes, thick and long, just like his. She was a petite one fifteen but stubborn and strong willed, like Arman' too.

"Terri...," she softly and hesitantly began. "There was an accident, a really bad accident and he was hurt and I don't know if he's gonna make it and I'm scared cause I can't do anything to make him better and..."

She broke again and I wasn't able to fully follow her. I gripped both of her shoulders.

"Pooh, wait...wait...calm down. You have to calm down and talk to me. Who was hurt? Slow down and breathe. Cory? Was Cory hurt? What accident are you talking about?"

"Arman'," she sobbed. "He hit a tree head on, completely totaled the car and now he's in the ICU, unconscious and they say he's not looking to good to survive the crash. Oh God, Terri...I don't know what I'd do if I lost my little brother..."

Her voice trailed off to me. I was frozen in time. Iced the moment she'd clearly spoken his name. Instantly, the world as I knew it had just ended. Thoughts turned to fear, fear turned to frenzy and frenzy turned to panic.

"Where is he? How did this happen? How did he hit a tree? Was the weather bad? What happened? How did this...oh God, no...no...Say this isn't real...say this isn't happening. It's just a dream, that's it; it's a dream...a bad dream. I'm gonna wake any minute now. Pinch me," I said, turning to Pooh and grabbing her by the arms.

I began to viciously shake her.

"Pinch me dammitt! Pinch me and wake me up! Tell me this isn't real, Pooh. Tell me the only man I ever loved isn't somewhere terribly hurt and possibly losing his life. Tell me! Please...please...tell me."

I collapsed onto her shoulders and cried. My tears intertwining with hers. Tears of fear, of misbelief and shock. A small cry began to intervene inside our sobs. It was our son AJ. We must have awakened him.

I sprang up from the couch, slowly fixed my robe and wiped my face. I couldn't let him see me that upset.

"I'd better go get him."

Pooh shook her head.

I took several deep breaths before my mind would allow my body to finally move.

"I'll be right back, okay?"

"Ok."

I stood in the door way of our son's bedroom, browsing the room and admiring the handy work of his father. Arman' had single handedly decorated his son's "palace" as he called it.

"Every prince should have one," he said, hammering away at AJ's mahogany and black dresser.

I walked over to the crib and gently pulled AJ into my arms. His yellow Sesame Street pj's were soak and wet. His eyes were wide open in disillusion as if he'd been entangled in the same

13

nightmare as I was, only a few moments ago.

Momma Jones, Arman's mother, once told me that babies could sense things that we adults couldn't. They could see things spiritually that we couldn't because babies were still pure and without sin. That they had a special connection with God. That truth would explain the fear I saw in our son's eyes at that moment. When I reached for him, he clutched my robe and held it intensely tight as if he were holding on for dear life.

I carried him over to the dressing table, grabbed him a change of clothing, his Nike overnight bag and headed back into the living room with Pooh. As I changed his diaper and dressed him, Pooh tried her best to fill me in on all she had heard about the accident.

"It was still light outside and I do know that there were no other cars involved. He wasn't drinking and the weather was fine. He was speeding though, according to the MP's (Military Police). He was flying somewhere in a major rush."

"Which way?" I asked her.

"Towards the Hood Road barracks."

"What's there?" I questioned.

"I don't know what or who's that way besides Cory. But that doesn't make any sense. Why would he be flying to see Cory, when Cory was the one who took Alicia to the hospital in the first place, right?"

"You're right, that doesn't make any sense. Cory was there

when she delivered the baby and everything. From my understanding, Cory even stayed with Alicia while Arman' went to give some blood for the baby. How's your mom handling all of this?"

"You know Ma; she immediately called Reverend Carter and headed up to the hospital. Then she sent me for you and the baby."

"And his wife? Has anybody talked to Alicia to find out what was going on?"

"She's not really up to talking to anyone. Her parents and her sister Punkin are there with her," she paused. "She said she needed some time alone with her family to try and grasp all the events of the day."

"I can certainly understand that. Poor thing, I actually feel sorry for her. She must be devastated."

I didn't like her, true, but I wouldn't wish this kinda pain on my worst enemy.

"A sick baby girl, now this. Any word on the baby?"

I was genuinely concerned for Arman's daughter. A part of him meant a part of me.

"She's not well. Like I said, I haven't been able to talk with Alicia to get the specifics but I do know she's not healthy, at all."

I went back into the nursery to gather up a few things for AJ and then went inside my bedroom to slip into something for the ride back to Fort Hood. I threw on a soft, pink velvet Nike sweat suit, a pair of flip flops and pulled my hair back into a ponytail.

On my dresser was a picture of Arman' wearing nothing but a pair of black Mickey Mouse boxers, lying across the very bed on which I was now sitting. I traced his face with my index finger.

Please don't let this be true, Lord. I need him, AJ needs him, and his baby girl needs him. Even his wife needs him. He has so much love surrounding him and so much to live for. Please don't take him away from us... from me. He's the only man I've every truly loved. I've gone through watching him love another woman, marry that woman and have a child with that woman, just to be apart of his life, in some way, any way. To share all I can with him and our son. I can't lose him now... please."

The tears began to fall again and I felt my heart sank into my stomach.

"Come on Terri, we gotta go. Momma's waiting for us," Pooh shouted from the living room.

"I'm coming," I replied in a broken voice.

I rose up off the bed, softly placed my lips to the frame and gently kissed it.

I'm coming Arman', just hold on for me...for AJ, we're coming.

I placed the picture back onto the dresser and headed out the room and down the hall. As I grabbed AJ from Pooh, he pointed to his daddy's picture on the mantel.

"Da..dada..da."

I kissed him on the forehead and softly whispered.

"I want him too, baby."

As I closed the door and locked it behind me, I couldn't help but wonder if I was closing the door to our lives together. Locking the treasure box that held the hope for our love and our future forever.

Chapter Two...Cory

"... *and I wish I never met her at all, even though I love her so and she got love for me. But she still belongs to some one else...*"

Carl Thomas laced the track as I sat there, reliving the last year-plus.

What the hell was I thinking?

I should've known better than to let a piece of pussy cloud my judgment when it came to the relationship between me and my nigga.

I fucked up bad this time. Arman' and I have been boyz way to fuckin' long for this shit. Now what? What the fuck am I gonna do now? Shit, the baby here now and ain't too much I can do besides kill that bitch. I told her dumb ass to get an abortion. Hell, she had the pussy on lock down anyway; he would've never known we was creepin' behind his back. But naw, she figured she could pull this shit off. Plant this baby on him and keep him away from Terri. Fuckin' broads, always tryin' to trap a nigga. Now I gotta deal with all this drama and bullshit that's about to go down.

I lay back on the mid-sized, navy blue sofa in my barracks room. The lights were down and I had an ice cold Miller Genuine Draft in my hand. It was almost Three AM. I sat there, staring up at the ceiling where I had the sun, the moon and the stars spread all throughout the room. They glowed in the dark and lit up my ceiling and the walls when the lights went out.

I'd always loved the galaxy. It reminded me of better days in my childhood when my dad and I used to sit outside in the courtyard of the Dallas projects where Arman' and I both grew up. Pops would always tell me how much he loved my moms, my brothers and me. He would go on and on about how lucky he felt to have a family to come home to every night after a hard days work.

How holding a family together was the most important accomplishment in a man's life. But of course, that was before the bastard ran out and left us for some young trick half his age.

Fuckin' women, every great man's noose around his fuckin' neck; day by day, slowly applying the pressure until one day, his dumb ass just stop breathing.

Anyways, I told Arman' that the display on my ceiling gave me the pleasure of feeling as if I was fuckin' out in space. I could still hear that nigga talkin' shit.

"Damn nigga, why you got all these damn stars and shit spread all over the walls and ceiling? You readin' Zodiac signs now? Tryin' to predict what the pussy gon' be like before you hit it?"

"Nigga, fuucckk you!"

I laughed.

"Shit, if I could scan the pussy first, I'd be one bad muthafucka, feel me? I always wanted to be the first pimp to hit a broad on the moon. But since a nigga ain't gettin' no calls from NASA these days, I figured I might as well live out the dream right here in my very own playa's nest."

Arman' shook his head and laughed.

"You the man playa, you the first and the last, beginning and the end."

"Sho' you right."

We laughed.

That nigga Arman' has always been the brother I always wanted and even though I already had two brothers, nobody could ever be closer to me than my nigga.

Damn, that nigga gon' kill me when he finds out. But I know that trick ain't gon' tell him cause her ass is in the fire too, just like mines. Hell, it ain't like I raped her ass or nothing,

I was trying to reason with myself.

And it wasn't like they were married when the shit started. Shit, she came on to me!

I sat back and reminised about the night I betrayed my best friend. Alicia was so pissed off at Arman' for what had happened earlier that afternoon. Arman's baby's momma, Terri went into labor and Arman' left Alicia at the altar to be with Terri for the delivery.

Later that night at her crib, I knocked on the bathroom door to check on Alicia and when she didn't answer, I opened the door to find her sitting on the toilet, dumping a pile of pills in her hands.

I sat down on the ledge of the white porcelain tub beside her.

"Now, what the fuck are you thinking about right now? Cause from where I'm sittin', well let's just say, this shit don't look to good."

"I know. No, I don't know. I just want to sleep Cory. I just wanna sleep the pain away," she said.

I honestly felt bad for her cause I knew she loved my boy but I also understood his position. Real men handle theirs and that means that sometimes women get caught up and hurt in the crossfire. But I liked Alicia, maybe a lil too much and I wasn't going to let her go out like that.

I took the pills from her hand.

"What's wrong with me Cory? I mean, tell me why am I not enough for him? How could he leave me on *my* special day to go and be with that, that hoe of his?"

I grabbed her hand and began removing the pills from her palm as I tried to talk some sense into her.

"Nothin's wrong with you baby, my nigga just had to go handle his business. You, as his woman has gotta both accept and respect that. Just cause he's mannin' up to his responsibility doesn't take anything away from how he feels about you. Shit, fo' real, you oughta want a nigga like that. As much as ya'll scream bout how all nigga's out here is dogs and don't man up to they responsibility, you got one of the ones who will. You got a good one. He knows he's got one of the good ones too. And as far as you being enough for him or any man for that matter, you can kill that noise cause you know you're 'enough for any man."

She smiled slightly.

"Really, Cory?"

"Fo' sho!"

She scooted closer to me.

"Don't stop, I need this. Keep talking to me. Do you really feel that way?"

"You know I do and so does he."

She tilted her head slightly towards me.

"Remember the first day I met you in the mall? You were with Arman' and you were trying to holla at me. You remember that? I remember... you wanted me, you wanted to touch me, feel me..."

I leaned back.

The fuck is wrong with her?

"Yeah...it was like that back then. But Alicia, you my nigga's gal now. I can't go out like that. If it was any other nigga, one I didn't give a fuck about, the panties would be at the ankles by now but I can't play my boy like that and the reality is... if ole girl had a better plug in her womb, you'd be his wife right about now."

"Yeah well, technically Cory, he dissed himself. He left me at the altar, remember?"

She gazed off at the ceiling.

"I never could compete with that bitch or that baby."

She began to cry. I placed my hand on her leg and squeezed her thigh.

"I feel like my entire world is fucking caving in around me. I can't be without him Cory, I can't. We've come too far for me to lose him to that bitch. I can't do this. I just wanna die if I can't have him."

"You talkin' crazy now. You done had a lil too much to drink and you trippin'. You know damn well that nigga love you more than life and would do anything in the world for you, you know that."

"Do I, Cory? Do I really know that? I mean, where is he right now? Does he really love me cause right about now I can't tell."

She wiped her face and scooted closer to me once again. She grabbed my hands and placed them around her waist.

"And anyways, I can't think about all that right now. Right now Cory, I just need to be held... would you hold me Cory?"

She began to kiss my neck.

"Just this once, Cory."

I tried to pull away from her again.

"Aey, aey...Alicia, this shit ain't cool. We can't do this."

"Like I said Cory, I need this, I need you right now, please don't say no, not tonight."

She started nibbling on my bottom lip.

"You do still want me...don't you Cory?"

She ran her hand across my thighs, unzipped my tux zipper and removed my jimmy from its resting place. I could no longer think straight. Shit, not with my upper head anyway.

Besides, I was the first one trying to hit her at the mall. I'm saying, what was I supposed to do? I'm a man first and once she had her lips around my jimmy, no more discussion was going down.

Yet, once the release came, I instantly regretted the shit and the fucked up part about it was, it wasn't all that great. But I kept it popping cause I knew she was available when I needed to release due to Arman' spending so much time with Terri and the new baby.

Divide and conquer, shit ain't that the American way?

I chuckled to myself.

Alicia wouldn't dare tell him. He'd drop her ass like a bad habit and head straight for Queen B.

He wanted Terri's ass all along anyway. So shit, in a way, I did his ass a favor.

I had to laugh out loud that time.

I picked up the remote and turned on the TV to help me unwind and hopefully fall asleep. Usually, I'd just call over a freak and fuck 'til I dozed off but I was really starting to feel Arman's sister Pooh. Another one I'd been trying to get with for the longest.

She was on the rebound from some sucka named Kevin and I slid in on the opportunity to wax that.

Get in where you fit in!

At first, all I set out to do was break her back. I didn't have plans on falling for her. Me and relationships were like kyrptonite but we'd been chillin' a lot more lately and I was seriously starting to dig her.

As I flicked through the television channels, I rested on the Fort Hood affiliate network, KWBC, who was dispatching the late local news. I figured I'd check the weather report for tomorrow and see if it would be cool for me to detail my jeep.

Gotta stay flossy.

"We have just learned the identity of the soldier involved in the head on collision early yesterday evening," the young white anchor man stated.

Great, I thought to myself.

Another dumb drunk ass nigga bites the dust.

"The driver has been identified by the Military Police as Specialist Arman' Letrey Jones of the 1st Infantry Division, here in Fort Hood."

I jumped to my feet, wondering if I'd just heard him correctly.

"The soldier hit a tree head on at the intersection of Jackson and Longbranch Rd. Reports clarify that there was no alcohol in the soldier's system at the time of the tragic crash but according to

25

MP's, the soldier was speeding in an excess of 70 miles per hour coming onto the base turnpike and may have lost control of his vehicle, rounding the dangerous corner. As you can see from these photographs taken earlier from our news crew, the late model Elauntra was totally crushed. At this hour, Specialist Jones is clinging to life at Irwin Army Hospital and doctors are giving little hope for survival. Our prayers go out to the soldier's family and friends."

I rushed over to the telephone and dialed the hospital to talk to his wife, Alicia. The nurse on the floor informed me that she wasn't taking any calls. I hung up and dialed the main switchboard and asked to speak to the doctor handling Arman' as a patient.

"Are you a relative?" the elderly nurse asked.

"Hell yeah!" I replied.

"I'm his brother."

She paused.

"I'm sorry but we don't have a brother listed for this patient. If you are not an immediate family member or his unit commander, we cannot divulge any information to you. I'm sorry, sir."

"Yeah, right."

I hung up.

"Ol' bitch!"

I called Momma Jones' house and let the phone ring about six times but no one answered. They must have been already at the hospital.

But why didn't they call me?

Maybe they figured Sarge had already told me. I felt lightheaded and sick to my stomach. I put the cordless phone onto the charger and plopped down onto the bed.

What the hell is goin' on man? Where the fuck were you goin' in such a hurry? Was it here? Naww, couldn't be...but why else would you be flying when you know how dangerous that damn turn is? What the hell was you thinkin'? And why won't that hoe Alicia take my fuckin' call? Is it possible?

I began to sweat. I needed to get to that hospital immediately and find out what was going on. I swooped up my keys and rushed out the door. As I was closing the door, the phone rung. I ignored it, figuring it was just one of my lil freaks, calling for a late night booty call. I couldn't even phantom the thought of pussy at that moment.

Hell, it was pussy that got me into this shit in the first damn place.

All I could think about was my boy, laying up there in the hospital. My ace-boon-coon, my homie, my brotha...down...like fo' flat tizes.

I got in my white Isuzu Jeep and floored it to the hospital, wondering what awaited me when I arrived. Whatever it was, I hoped it wasn't those fuckin' blood tests!

Chapter Three...Terri

"...the storms of life will blow. They're sure to come and go. They meet us all at a time, when we're calm and doing fine..."

Once Pooh and I arrived at the hospital, I left her standing in the lobby and stopped at the pay phone to call Cory. Pooh wasn't sure if he'd been told about Arman's accident or not. I let the phone ring several times before hanging up. Maybe he was already upstairs with Arman'. I'm sure Alicia would've called him by now and told him the tragic news.

I returned the quarter to my purse and walked to the lobby where Pooh and AJ were waiting.

"No answer. He must be upstairs already."

We took the elevator to the same fourth floor intensive care unit that Willie, Arman's and Pooh's father had died in close to a year ago from cancer.

As soon as we stepped off the elevator, we were greeted by Rev. Carter and his wife.

"Where's Ma?" Pooh asked.

Rev. Carter was a stylish, fifty something year old, handsome preacher. He was decked out in a pin striped suit with blue Gators.

"She's inside with your brother. She's been waiting for you both."

"Is Cory inside also?" Pooh questioned.

28

"No, I haven't seen him."

He hugged Pooh and kissed her on the cheek.

"We're all praying for him."

Then he turned to me. A hint of surprise on his face at seeing me standing there.

"Hello, Ms. Lambert. I haven't seen you since...well you know."

Rev. Carter was referring to me interrupting Alicia and Arman's wedding ceremony. My labor had begun at three am the previous night but I refused to go to the hospital until I'd seen Arman' marry out of my life forever, or so I thought. My labor had gone to the next level and my water had broken during the ceremony. Arman' had left his wife-to-be's side to come along with me to the hospital. I really did want him to stay at the chruch and move on with his life but he insisted on being there to see our child born into this world.

He hadn't seen or heard from me in months. He knew I was pregnant but he had already made it clear that he wasn't ready to be a father. He'd expressed it in a letter he had written while he was deployed in the field. He had written it to Alicia but he'd made a mistake and placed it in the wrong envelope addressed to me.

When I received it, my world came tumbling down. So I did what I always do at the first blow of pain, I ran. I didn't even know about Alicia. I thought I was the only one in his life. To find out otherwise, hurt like hell.

I wiped a smear of drool from AJ's mouth, politely smiled and addressed Rev. Carter.

"Hello, Reverend Carter."

"The wife and I can keep the little one out here with us while you go in to see his father."

I looked to Pooh and she nodded her head in agreement.

"It wouldn't be good for him to see his daddy like...like..."

She began to cry again.

I handed Mrs. Carter the baby, kissed him, took Pooh by the arm and headed down towards Arman's room. The hospital smell alone made me want to puke. As I opened the brown oak door, I almost fainted. There were machines all around him and tubes running from almost every part of his body. His head was wrapped up and even in the distance; I could see how badly his face was bruised. There was a respirator hooked to his mouth and they had a brace around his neck. One of his legs were in a cast.

Momma Jones was sitting beside him in a chair, unaware of our presence. Knowing Momma J, she was using her direct line to God in prayer.

Pooh began to holler, "Oh God... no... no... oh God... NNNOOOOO..."

"Pooh, Pooh please, you have to calm down. We can't upset him."

I was crying as well but I was trying to stay in control at the same time.

"Take a deep breath; come on... Momma Jones needs us and so does Arman'. He'll get upset if he feels us upset. I know he knows we're here, I can feel him. So slow down, breathe and let's go give him a big, big kiss."

She slowly nodded her head.

I took her by the hand as we both nervously began walking towards the bed. The closer we got, the more I felt as if I was inside the twilight zone. It didn't seem as if I was moving at all. Yet, in no time at all there I was, standing beside Momma J, looking down at my badly bruised up soul mate.

"Momma J, we're here," I told her softly as I touched her shoulder. It amazed me that she was so deep into prayer that Pooh's outburst hadn't disturbed her at all.

She raised her head and smiled.

"Awww, bless you chil', bless you. I'm shol' is glad you made it. Where's the baby?" she asked, looking around.

"Rev. Carter and his wife is keeping an eye on him out in the waiting room. They thought it would be best."

"I guess so, fo' now anyways. Manni' needs to feel love from those closest to him right now."

"Have the doctor's been in yet, Ma?" Pooh asked. She was standing over Arman', afraid to move or touch him.

"They have roun's in bout twenty minutes or so. We'll talk to 'em then. I called yo' sista's. They's waitin' fo' word from me befo' comin' all the way down here."

"Where's Alicia? Won't the doctor's let her come down? And where's Cory?" I asked.

"I don't what's goin' on with Alicia. She hasn't come down here yet. The nurse say she's probably still exhausted from the difficult labor with the baby. Don't know where Cory is either. God only knows what that young man is up to at almost fo' in the mo'ning."

Pooh's face tensed up slightly. Momma J didn't know that Cory and Pooh were in a relationship. Don't get me wrong, Momma J loved Cory like one of her own but she too knew he wasn't worth a quarter, woman wise.

"Now, now Momma Jones, once I found out, there's no other place I'd be besides right here."

We turned to see Cory coming through the door. Pooh ran to his arms and broke down again. Momma Jones grabbed my hand.

"He's gon' be alright chil'. God has already promised me so."

I kneeled down beside her.

"He promised you? How?"

I wasn't raised in a church and my parents taught me nothing about God. With all I had gon' through, I found it difficult to believe that there was someone watching over me and allowed all those horrible things to happen to me as a child. Things so bad, they forced me into an early marriage just to get away.

"He promised me in His Word. In the book of Psalms, written by David, one of the most loved Men by God. Psalms 23 verse four and five states, "*yea, thou I walk through the valley of the shadow of death, I will fear no evil, for thou art with me. Thy rod and thy staff, they comfort me.* Do you know what that means, chil'?"

I shook my head, no.

"It means that my son has no reason to be afraid and neither do we. God is with him and He will bring him outta the devil's evil grip. Satan comes but to kill, steal and destroy. But he won't get my chil', no sir-re! I'm gon' fight this here war in the spirit realm. You've gotta fight too."

"But...I, I don't..."

She patted my hand.

"Don't worry chil', He knows you don't know. When the time comes, he'll show you."

To be honest, I felt a little more relaxed then.

"Did you find out exactly what happened yet, Ma? I mean nobody called me. I found out watchin' the news," Cory stated.

"Oh Cory, I'm so sorry. We tried to call and when we got no answer, we figured Alicia had already told you," I said.

Cory waved his hand.

"Don't matter now, I'm here. So you find out anythin'?"

"Nothin' much, just that he was flyin' somewhere's in a

33

hurry. He's been out since the crash, so nobody knows what was goin' on in his head at the time." Momma J stated.

"Alicia ain't say nothin'?" he asked.

"She hasn't talked to nobody," Pooh answered.

"What's up with that? You don't think they had it out or something before he left the hospital, do you?" she questioned.

"I don't know," I said. "Cory, weren't you here with them? Did you sense anything strange? I mean why would he be speeding towards the Hood Road Barracks?"

"I left shortly after he got here, so I don't know what might've transpired after I bounced."

"You think he was coming to tell you something? I mean, if he were majorly upset with her or about anything, he'd come straight to you, right?"

I was trying to grasp some type of understanding as to why the man I loved was lying here, fighting for his life.

"I 'spose so," he answered. "That's usually the move but lately, that's been yo' territory, right?"

I caught the sarcastic meaning behind that but I let it slide. Emotions were running high and Cory never did care too much for me. He always blamed me, in my opinion for Alicia's unhappiness and Arman's unwillingness to stay totally committed to her.

As I opened my mouth to respond, in walked a frail elderly nurse and a tall, stocky white man I assumed was the doctor handling Arman's case. They approached us cautiously.

"Good morning folks, I assume you're the family?"

"Yeah," Cory stated. "This is his mother Ms. Jones, This is his sister right here and this is his..."

He glanced to me.

"This is his son's mother."

"And you are," the little short nurse asked.

"I'm his best...I'm his section chief."

"And he's family. Anythang you need to say, you go right ahead say it," Momma J co-signed.

"I see. Well, I was the attending physician on duty when they brought your son into the ER. We stabilized his vitals, did a few necessary procedures and sent him up to the ICU. The anesthesiologist will be later to remove the respirator since his vitals are holding within the normal range. He's very lucky to be alive. He was compressed underneath the metal of the dashboard. His right lung collapsed, which we took care of in the ER by inflating a small balloon with air and inserting it into his lungs. I'll be honest, I didn't expect him to hang on this long but that in itself is very encouraging news. Also, there's no sign of internal bleeding which is comforting news when you're involved in a crash like that.

He did suffer a few broken ribs, a broken leg and a lot of head trauma, as you can see. It'll take some days before we know the extent of it. However, I'm concerned about some swelling he has around his spinal cord."

"Why? What does that mean?" Pooh asked.

He gripped his clipboard.

"Well, to put it to you realistically, the swelling could be hiding a severed portion of his spine. And that would mean possible paralysis. Possibly, from the neck down."

Pooh and I broke down in unison. Cory squeezed both of our shoulders. And through tears of his own, asked the doctor about Arman's head trauma.

"Well at this point, he's comatose. He's not responding to visual stimulation at all."

"You saying, he's a vegetable?" I asked in horror.
"Until he makes his way back to us...I'm afraid so. This can be very difficult to put a time line on. It's basically up to his brain and his will power."

Pooh buried her head in Cory's chest.

"Why is this happening Cory, why?"

I broke away from the pack and walked over to Arman'. I wondered if he could feel me there. I leaned down into his ear.

"I love you Arman', more than life itself, you know that. And even if you can't hear me. I know you can feel my love flowing through my touch. Please come back to me, to us all."

I tried to maintain composure while I waited for him respond. With a squeeze of my hand or movement of some kind. It came in the form of Alicia. The nurse had her waiting outside until they could tell us what was going on. The doctor and his colleagues excused themselves as Punkin, Alicia's sister, accompanied them inside.

Alicia was in a wheelchair dressed in her blue hospital gown, eyes swollen shut from crying. The day must have been so hard on her. As she entered, Pooh rushed over to her side.

"I'm so glad you're here, maybe now we can shed some light on all this and get to the bottom of this. Are you okay? We were so worried about you? How's the baby? I know this is all so overwhelming for you."

They exchanged kisses as I gently squeezed Arman's hand before releasing it. I didn't want to disrespect Alicia. As Punkin wheeled her closer to everyone, she shot Cory a look that could kill.

He softly spoke to Punkin and leaned down to kiss Alicia but she pulled back.

What was up with that? Maybe she's trippin' cause Pooh was clinging onto Cory.

At one time, Cory and her sister Punkin had been an item, according to her. According to him, he'd just hit it whenever he felt like it.

Momma Jones rose up from her seat to greet Alicia.

"Hey Baby, how's you feelin'?"

"I'm fine mom, I'm just so tired from worrying about Arman' and the baby."

"How is my gran'child?"

Alicia looked to Cory. A moment of intense friction passed between them.

"She's hanging in there. I'm sure she'd be better if she could see her father."

She looked to Cory again, this time it was her who shot him daggers through her eyes.

What the hell is going on around here?

Pooh walked over to Cory and wrapped herself back inside his arms. Punkin rolled Alicia to Arman's bedside and I extended my hand to her. She snickered at my outstretched palm.

"You just couldn't wait to run here like the perfect little mistress could you?"

I put my hand to my chest. Amazed that in such a life changing ordeal, she could still be so hateful. We both shared a common bond with Arman'. We both loved him and we both, or so I thought, felt that his recovery was the most important thing at the moment.

"Aey, Alicia, don't start that shit up in here!" Cory demanded.

"I'm right though, ain't I Cory? She couldn't wait to be by his side. *My* man's side, *my* husband's side..."

"Alicia you cut out this here mess, right now! I won't have it in here...not while my son is ailin'!" Momma Jones spurted out.

I couldn't believe she had the nerve to come at me like that. And here I was, feeling sorry for this heifer and she wanted to get jiggy. Puff her chest out and shit.

"Don't play dumb huzzie, you'd get in any way you could fit in. When you gon' get it? It ain't gon' happen between ya'll! Hell, he's layin' here because of you!"

The entire room got quiet and still. My heart stood on edge and my breath got caught inside my chest.

Why would she say that? What had I done to cause Arman' to crash his car?

I looked to Pooh, Momma Jones and even to Cory. All were watching me, waiting for me to explain. I looked to Alicia, awaiting the same.

"Me? How is this my fault? How did I cause him to get hurt?"

"He was pissed off and on his way to tell Cory about some test results he'd gotten back."

Cory's eyes almost popped out of his head. He cleared his throat.

"What results?" he questioned.

Alicia began to wave her hand all wild and crazy.

"You know the ones he had done on the baby..."

Cory almost choked.

"AJ," Alicia continued. "Remember, he had the tests done on AJ because he was having doubts if AJ was his son after the way you ran off the second time."

"Oh...oh yeah, those tests," Cory sputtered. "Well, why

was he rushin' to tell me that?"

"I don't know, he came back from the lab pissed. You know they sent him there to provide some blood for our daughter," she said, rolling her eyes at me.

"So, he picked up those results while he was there. He came back to me in a blinding rage and said he had to talk to you about it."

"What did the results say?" Pooh asked.

I looked at her in disbelief. Surely all of this was some kind of mistake. At best, a sick joke. Surely if what she was saying was true, those results indeed proved that AJ was his son.

Arman' and I had a beautiful relationship. We were in love with each other and spent so much time together. We talked about everything. If he had any questions, we would have discussed them, I knew that for sure.

"I don't know," Alicia insisted.

"But he was furious with her. And now look at my husband! Lying there, fighting for his life because of you. Get out!" she spit out.

"Alicia, this is..."

"GET OUT!! I want you out of this room, right now!"

I backed up to the wall, feeling dizzy.

Tests, doubts, AJ, paternity...Arman' couldn't have doubted AJ's paternity. He knew better than to think anything like that.

The entire family was still looking at me except for Cory,

who was looking down at the ground. I needed some air. I felt like I was about to suffocate.

"Ex...excuse me guys...um...I'm gonna go and check on AJ."

"Yeah, you do that. You go and check on *your* son!" Alicia snapped.

I walked down the hall to the waiting room and AJ was still asleep on Mrs. Carter's lap. As I stood there staring at the spitting image of Arman', my heart ached at the very thought of him doubting AJ's paternity. Suddenly, guilt began to overwhelm me. If this really was my fault over some incorrect test results...then that meant it was because of me, that the man I love, lay there... comatose.

I began to cry, wondering what he might have been thinking in the moments before he hit that tree.

Oh God...I wondered what he thought of me...he thought I had betrayed him and I could only imagine...better yet, I preferred not too...

Chapter Four...Cory

Cool, she played that shit off, yet in her own little cunning way, she let me know the information I came for. He knew, fuck! And he was speeding my way to confront me with the shit!

I stepped over to the window.

W*hat would the family think? Ma J and Pooh would definitely flip the fuck out!*

Lately, Pooh and I had been kicking it solo and once this comes out; I could definitely kiss our shit goodbye.

Terri, God... she would definitely love this. It would definitely prove that all I was, was a dog ass nigga who deserved to be somewhere getting' neutered. Damn!

The more I watched Alicia go for her Oscar, the more I began to boil inside.

She was flung onto his arm, crying as if they had the perfect marriage.

"Baby, I love you. Please say something to me. Please... wake up Arman'... our baby's waiting to see you. She wants her daddy. Please, Boo... wake up... Arman'... please..."

She was pouring in on too. I mean, no doubt, she really loved the nigga but damn!

Pooh bought into that shit hook-line-and-sinker. She squeezed my arm.

"Poor Alicia, I feel so bad for her, don't you?"

"Yeah," I said, sarcastically. "I'm heart broken."

Pooh looked up to me.

"Was what Alicia said about Arman' having doubts and doing blood tests on AJ really true?"

"I'm not one hundred percent sure. You know that nigga loves lil' man more than life. If it is true, I can see him flyin' into a rage," I said.

Hey, I had to try to keep her thrown off until I found out exactly what Alicia's trick ass had told him.

Pooh looked to Arman'.

"I can't believe that, I just can't. There's no way AJ isn't his...son."

It was getting a little uncomfortable for me, discussing all that biological bullshit and when Pooh asked me to accompany her upstairs to see Arman's new baby girl, who was actually mines, I freaked.

"Umm, I can't right now baby. I gotta go and let the COC (chain of command) know what's what but I'll be back as soon as I can. Ok?"

"You sure honey?"

"I promise, as soon as I can, aight?"

"Ok."

"You gon' be aight?" I asked.

"Yeah, I'll be fine. You go ahead. I'll keep you posted if anything significant happens."

I kissed both her and Momma J. In my mind, I dreaded for that call to come.

God, what must have been runnin' through my nigga's mind?

I felt like shit, in every sense of the word. I had to get outta there.

I walked over and leaned into Alicia's ear.

"I need to talk to you."

"Go to hell! There's not a damn thing for us to talk about. He was so mad at you. He was coming to kill you. You need to stay the fuck away from me, our daughter..."

She looked around to see if anyone could hear her.

"And Arman'...and pray he dies cause if he don't, your ass will!"

I glanced into her eyes and saw nothing but coldness. It was at that moment I knew she had told him everything about us. I rose up, shaking my head in disgust. I couldn't believe her. I watched as she rolled her eyes and returned to her staring role with the family.

I walked outside the room and bumped directly into Terri.

"Cory, can I ask you something? Was that true? Please, I need to know. I need to hear it from you. If anybody knows, it would be you. Did Arman' really have doubts about being AJ's father?"

"Look at yo' track record and answer that fo' yo' damn self. I'm out!"

She called after me but I kept walking. I didn't wanna talk to nobody, I just wanted to get the hell away from there. I dipped into the stairwell and headed for my car.

While driving in search of a liquor store, Glen Lewis' **It's Ain't Fair,** hit me below the belt. *"...and I trusted you and this is what I get in return. You were like a brother to me, now I see you were just waiting your turn. While I was out at work, ya'll was doin' dirt, stealin' my heart away. It ain't fair..."*

I copped a case of MGD's and decided I was neither ready to go back to the barracks nor back to the hospital. I hit Hwy 35 and headed for the hood Arman' and I grew up in together.

The streets still looked the same. The buildings still sprayed with the graffiti we'd done as kids. New generations adding to it with the memories of fallen street soldiers.

I pulled over on Meramec St. and parked in front of our old project building. I sat down on the same old wooden bench we use to sit on and chill for hours at a time. I sat back and thought of all the shit we'd done together, the conversation we'd had the day my daddy left.

"You know man," I began. "Everything he has ever said to me sittin' out here was a lie. He was just pacifying me while at the same time, he was doin' everything under the sun to tear this family apart. I hate that nigga. I hope I never see his punk ass again!"

"Naw dawg, you don't mean that. You just mad right now. I know you hurt but..."

"Hurt? Nigga, I ain't hurt. I'm a man, I don't get hurt. I just hate his ass, that's all."

"Cory, its okay to be the man and still be hurt. I hurt, cause I never met my dead beat ass daddy. And I'm mad at yours for leavin' too. He's the only daddy I've known. I'm hurt but I don't hate him. And you don't either."

He saw the tears rolling down my face. I tried to quickly brush them off. The man had left me to become the man of the house at age eleven. I had to take on the challenge and step up to the plate. Arman' scooted closer to me and put his hand on my shoulder.

"Its cool man, you can cry in front of me. We boys and we gon' always be boys. See that car over there? What's wrong with it?"

I raised my head to see a blue Chevy Nova parked across the lot.

"All its tires flat," I said.

He held out his hand.

"That's us nigga. We gon' always be down like that. Like them fo' flat tires."

I slapped my hand down inside his and he punched me in the arm.

"Let me find out you soft nigga, cryin' and shit."

We laughed.

We stuck together like glue since that day. Nothing nor no one could come between us. Yeah, we had our spats and shit but nothing a good "slap boxing match" couldn't solve.

We've gone through our share of women together too. I was always the outgoing one, who always got both who and what I went after. Arman' was the soft spoken, polite one. His moms had raised him to be a gentleman; mine had raised me to believe that they were all home wrecking hoes.

A wave of emotion took over me. I had allowed my thirst for conquering women cloud my judgment and now, here I was, halfway through a case of MGD's, realizing the depths of my mistakes.

I finally broke down, heavily. I cried tears of regret, tears of anger, and tears of fear...tears of pain. The pain was so intense. I drank and drank but nothing could numb the pain I was feeling. It was the kind of pain I had only known once before in my life...that night on the stoop.

A shadow approached me from beyond the Garden playground. It was one of our old partners named Earl, who we called Earl-the-Pearl, as kids.

We slapped dap and he sat down beside me to shoot the breeze with me. The conversation turned to Arman' and I began to explain all the in's and outs of what happened.

"Damn nigga, that's fucked up. Here," he said, reaching down into his pocket, "I got somethin' to take yo' mind off all yo' troubles."

He produced a finely rolled joint, lit it up and handed it to me. It had been years since I'd gotten high but as stressed out as I was, I said, "fuck it." I inhaled it, slowly yet strongly and tried to forget all that had transpired in the last twenty four.

This joint was like no other I'd smoked before. It was different...better. Slowly, I smoked another and another, until all of my pain was gone. Earl-the-Pearl had hooked me up...or shall I say, the joint had hooked me...

ℭhapter Five...Terri

I took the elevator down to the first floor and made my way down the cold corridor to the hospital chapel. Slowly, I opened the grey metal door. Outside of Arman's wedding and a few funerals, I had never stepped foot inside a church before. It just simply wasn't a part of my world. Yet, I felt the need to try.

Inside, the atmosphere was warm and soothing. Tall white candles were lit all around the altar. The infamous Cross I'd seen atop of churches everywhere was embedded in gold. Families were spread all about, praying for miracles, I presumed.

My heart beat increased as I slowly walked up and kneeled down beside a young black soldier. He was crying. Bearing his soul to a God I'd never known.

"Are you okay?" I asked him.

He looked to me and softly spoke through his broken voice.

"No, I'm not. My wife is upstairs, dying. She has cervical cancer. The doctors say this is probably her last night with us."

I placed my hand upon his shoulder.

"I'm so sorry. How long have you been married?"

"Just eleven months. It came from no where. Snuck up on her and stole her life from us all."

He paused to collect himself.

"She sent me down here to pray; only I don't know what to say to God. How about "thanks" God, for taking her away from me and fixing it so she couldn't have a baby to leave behind. "Thank you" for cheating me out of an entire family. Is that what you want me to say Samantha? Cause that's what I feel!"

He bowed over, crying uncontrollably for a couple of minutes. I patted him on his back in an effort to soothe him. He wiped his face, gathered himself and stood to his feet.

"You go ahead, ma'am. Maybe He'll listen to you cause He sure didn't listen to my Sam. All these nights she spent in church, praying to get better. And for what? Huh?"

Slowly, he turned around and walked out of the chapel in a defeated state of existence. I felt so bad for him. I actually understood his pain.

Why does God allow bad things to happen to good people?

I couldn't pray. The time just wasn't right for me.

I stood up to leave the chapel. As I passed by, a small older white woman, sitting on one of the benches grabbed my wrist. I jumped because she had startled me when she reached for me. She looked up into my eyes and sternly said, "The truth is in the darkness."

"Excuse me Ma'am, what did you say?"

"The truth lies in the darkness," she repeated. "Bring him back from the darkness to the light and the truth shall be revealed. Thus sayeth the Lord."

"Bring who?"

She didn't answer.

"Ma'am, what darkness? What light?"

She just continued to sit there, silently staring at the Bible on her lap. I glanced down at the pages and highlighted paragraph that read, "And in that day, you will call on Me and I will answer."

Call on You? How? Tell me how!

I stood there waiting for the answers to come, nothing happened. Frustrated, I clutched my hands and headed out the door.

When I reached the ICU on the fourth floor, the elevator opened and I noticed a slew of doctors and nurses running into Arman's room. I instantly took off, leaving my flip flops behind at the elevator doors. Loud, horrible screams were coming from inside. As I rushed through the crowd, the doctor was instructing his team.

"Hit him with 300 volts."

"What's happening? Somebody, tell me what's happening," I started screaming to no one in particular.

"What's wrong with him? What are they doing to him?"

Momma J grabbed me and pulled me back outside the room.

"His heart stopped beatin' fo' a minute when they took him off the respirator," she said, looking inside the room.

"But, he'll be back. He's just spendin' a lil time with God is all."

"He's dead? He can't be! Arman'..."

51

I tried to break away from Momma J's grip and rush back inside his room. She wouldn't let me go.

"Now you calm down chil'! God's got this here thang all unda control. The best thang we can do fo' him is pray."

There was that word again.

Pray what? Pray how?

All I could think about was the young soldier, kneeling at the altar downstairs in the chapel.

He was right, what's the use?

Then the paragraph highlighted in the older woman's Bible flashed before my eyes.

And in that day, you will call on Me and I will answer.

Momma J had already begun praying as the doctor again, yelled inside the room.

"350...come on son...don't go out like this."

I slowly and insecurely bowed my head. With tears frantically falling, I whispered.

"I don't really know who it is I'm praying to right now. But if You really do exist, can You please bring Arman' back to us. Even if all this is my fault, I'd rather have him alive and hate me, than to never see him again. Please...God...don't let him die."

As I softly continued to plead for his life, my tears began to dry and my heartbeat slowed down. When I opened my eyes, the doctor was coming towards us, wiping his forehead with his handkerchief.

"We had a scare there for a minute but he apparently still had something to live for."

I glanced over at our son sleeping so peacefully in the midst of the storm.

How could he think that AJ wasn't his?

"Didn't I tell you chil', you's gotta have faith."

She winked her eye at me.

"We've got him stabilized for now. We'll beef up our watch on him and keep a closer eye on his vitals. By the way, his eyes are open."

"Really?" I asked excitedly.

"Yes, but I must warn you, it's routine with some patients who's flat lined and we've had to hit'em with over 300 volts of electricity."

"Oh," I said disappointed.

"Thank you anyways Doctor for bringing him back to us."

"That's my job Ma'am."

We walked inside the room. All of us, standing around his bed. We were watching his eyes for movement, some sign of life but nothing came. He just stared blankly into space.

Tears began to roll down my face again. Momma J squeezed my hand and told me not to worry. He'd be fine. I prayed she was right, if only for a moment. It was all I needed to explain to him that those test results were wrong. That I'd slept with no one other than him since the first moment I'd laid eyes on him.

I looked down and promised him within my soul that I'd make this right...if only given the chance. All I needed was a chance.

𝕮hapter Six...Arman'

The darkness has faded. Light has emerged and along with it, figures, shadows, machines and people. These women, all looking down so sadly at me. I couldn't narrow my eyes to focus in either one in particular, yet I could feel one of them lodged immensely inside my soul. She was connected to me in some way, I just didn't know how.

I tried to dig through my mental rolodex to see where I knew her from but I couldn't recall anything past that moment. She leaned down and placed a kiss on my check. For some reason, I desperately wanted to reach up and wipe the tears from her eyes but nothing happened. My body wouldn't follow my heart.

*Awwwww...pain...*there was a strong, sharp pain, piercing inside my head. A flash of a still picture appeared in front of me. Leaves, it was a shadow of leaves. The image only lasted for a moment, then it was gone. I wondered what it had meant.

I lay there, watching the three women although my eyes couldn't move from that one spot. The smaller one pacing the floor endlessly.

It came again...the pain...stronger this time...the sound of fluid, rushing through my ears. A sharp pain shot down my back and through my arms. It was so intense; it brought tears to my eyes. With the flow of tears, my eyes began to blink.

"Momma, did you see that? His eyes are blinking! And he's..."

The woman voice got softer and more broken in structure.

"Ma, is he crying? Is he in that much pain? Why is he crying? Oh, Manni, please don't cry."

"It's alright chil', tears or not. God is answerin' my prayers. He's always faithful and right on time."

Ma? As in mother? Is she my mother?

She certainly looked as if she had a gentle and sweet mothering spirit. But if she was my mother, how come I couldn't remember her? I didn't recognize any of them. Certainly I'd remember those so close to me. Especially my mother and the pretty one I felt so drawn to.

The pain came again, stronger and stronger.

"Uuuhhhhhh...pain...the pain..."

It was sound. My thoughts made a sound.

"Manni, oh my God Manni, you're talking," the smaller woman screamed as she turned around to embrace the older woman.

"I gotta go get the doctor! Oh my God, he's awake!"

Manni? She called me Manni, is that my name?

The older woman leaned in and kissed my forehead.

"That's my baby boy. I knews you'd pull through. You'd always been as stubborn as a bull. God wasn't ready fo' you yet son. He knew we needed you here wit' us. Oh, I love you so much Manni. And we's gon' be right here wit' cha, all the way."

She was my mother. But why couldn't I remember her? I didn't know her. I didn't know any of them. I didn't even know my own name and no matter how hard I tried, I couldn't remember what happened to land me in the hospital.

I looked up at all of them. The younger woman, the beautiful one, said nothing. She just slowly backed away from the bed, stumbling into the wall behind her. A cloud of sadness and fear hovered above her.

What's with her? Ain't she glad I'm alright?

Her spirit still seemed so broken and defeated. Something about her eyes told me there was something between us. That she was an important part of whatever life I had.

The petite woman came back into the room with the doctor and a nurse on her heels.

"What happened?" he asked as he placed an instrument to my chest and listened to my heart beat. He flashed a light into my eyes.

The small woman started talking a mile a minute. He shined the light into my eyes again and I blinked repeatedly.

"Pain," I dryly whispered. "Pain."

"Well hello soldier. Glad to see you're still among us and pulling through. You gave all of us quite a scare for a minute there. Don't try to talk right now. Your throat is still a little agitated from the respirator. You're experiencing pain so intensely because we haven't given you any pain medication. There was no need to medicate you while your brain was shut down. The fact that you're experiencing it now is a very good sign. Let's test your blood flow to your limbs before the nurse administers a little Dorsal to you through your IV. I'm gonna hit you on your limbs one by one and you tell me if you feel anything. Remember, don't try to talk, tell me by blinking your eyes, got it? Blink now if you understand me."

I blinked my eyes.

First, he hit the right side of my neck, I blinked. Then he hit me on my shoulders, I blinked again. My chest followed, then my arms and down to my fingers. I blinked consistently with each touch of the metal gavel onto my skin.

Then he moved down to my thighs. My eyes remained open. He hit me again and again. I didn't blink, I couldn't. I didn't feel anything. The only way I knew he had touched me was by sight, not feeling.

"Go ahead Nurse McAllister; give him 50mgs of Dorsal every two hours."

He sighed and looked at the women.

"May I speak to you all outside in the hallway.

They all nodded. He patted me on the arm and told me to hang in there.

The beautiful one turned back to look at me once more before leaving the room. I saw panic in her facial expression and I knew what he wanted to say to them wasn't good news.

What happened to me? Why couldn't I feel him hitting my legs?

As soon as I was able to talk, I'd make it my business to find out what happened... and the beautiful one would be the one to tell me.

Chapter Seven...Terri

As we walked towards the door, I glanced back at Arman'. He was awake and I could tell by his eyes, the way they stared through me and not at me, he knew something.

Was he thinking about the blood tests?

I was praying he wasn't cursing the day he met me in his mind. I couldn't wait for the chance to talk to him alone. I had to explain how crazy the idea of AJ not being his sounded. Arman' had to know how much I loved him. He just had too.

Outside the room, the doctor's face was very tense.

"He's gonna be alright now, right doctor? I mean, he's awake and trying to talk. You said it's great that he's feeling pain, right?"

Pooh was so excited.

"Well," he began. "It's a very good sign that he's up and trying to talk. The soreness will subside in a few days. We'll run some more tests on him throughout the days ahead to see how much damage, if any, the concussion caused. As for the pain he's experiencing, well..."

He paused and massaged his temples.

"What is it doctor? What about the pain? You said it was a good sign. That's what you said, right?" I questioned.

"Yes, I did say that and it is good. The bad thing is that he's only feeling it in his upper body."

60

"What does that mean?" I asked.

He stared down as he jotted some notes onto his clipboard.

"Remember I told you I was concerned about the swelling around his spinal cord? Well, I'm gonna have to order some tests in the next hour or so but the initial diagnosis will be that he's possibly paralyzed from the waist down."

"No... no... that ain't true... that ain't true! Not my baby! My baby's gon' get up and walk outta here!" Momma J spit out sternly.

"You here me? My God is able to do all thangs. My chil' ain't no paralyzed! You fix him!" she ordered him as she began to cry.

I had never seen Momma Jones cry before, not even at Arman's father's funeral. She was always so strong but this was her baby boy and she adored Arman' with all her heart. We all felt her pain.

"You fix him!"

"I'll do my best Ma'am. In the meantime, why don't you go on home and get some rest. You've been here all night. It's 10 am. Why don't you all come back in a couple of hours and I should have some information for you then. I'm very sorry and I'll do my best for him."

"He's right, Ma. You been up all night. I'll go up and tell Alicia and I'll call Cory. Rev. Carter can take you home. Terri," she turned to me.

"You need to go with Ma. I'll stay here and once you've rested, we can switch, okay? We'll take turns so someone will always be here with him. Go on and get some sleep."

I shook my head, no.

"You're no good to him like this Terri. He needs you of all people to be strong. Not just for him but for AJ. Go home and get some rest and I'll call you if anything happens. Rest and then we'll trade."

Finally, I relented. Hopefully by the afternoon, the doctor would have something to tell us. I wanted to go back inside the room to see him again. Look into his eyes and tell him how much I loved him but I decided it would be best if I waited until we could be alone. I didn't know what to expect from him and that scared me.

I'd come back when it was my time to sit with him. I couldn't bare the thought of the family I had come to love as my own, knowing what he thought of me right before he crashed his car.

I grabbed AJ and we headed down the hallway to the elevator. Rev Carter and his wife offered to take AJ for the day and allow me to get some sleep. That sounded good to me. Mrs. Carter looked at me and smiled.

"It'll be alright honey. It's all just a test. One you've gotta pass in order to have a testimony about it one day. Just have faith, He'll do the rest."

I nodded my head and prayed she way right. For only Supreme Power could fix the mess that was about to unfold.

Chapter Eight...Cory

I turned over and looked at the clock on Earl's wall...10:29 am.

Shit, I missed PT(physical training). BC(battalion commander), gon' kill my ass! Fuckin' wit' Earl!

My phone was ringing. I rubbed my eyes and stared at the unfamiliar digits. The number was from the hospital. Damn, it was the call I dreaded. I flipped open the phone and dryly answered.

"Holla."

"Hey you, it's me, Pooh. You won't believe what I'm about to tell you."

"Oh yeah? Try me."

"Arman's awake."

A knot instantly tied up in my stomach.

"What?"

"Yes honey, he's not fully talking yet. But he started mumbling something about pain, so the doctor gave him some medication. He's a little groggy but he's awake."

"No shit, that's tight... that's aight. I'm glad. I was really worried about my nigga."

Her voice began to crack.

"Yeah, we were too. He flat lined a few..."

"What? Flat lined, how the fuck that happen? Where the hell was the doctor?"

"Cory, calm down, it's okay. They had removed his respirator so he could try to breathe on his own. He was doing well but then his heart stopped beating. It was after that though, that his eyes opened. I don't know what he was thinking about but he starting crying."

"Damn... for real?"

"Yeah, I'm right here beside him. You wanna say something to him? I know he won't answer you back but I know he'd love to hear your voice."

"You think so?"

I doubted that very seriously. Pooh didn't know what I knew.

"Yeah, you're his best friend. More so, his brother than anything. Of course he'd wanna hear your voice."

She cut me like a knife with that statement.

Why couldn't I have been the brother to him that he'd always been to me? I couldn't think of a time in our life long friendship when Arman' had crossed me. Over some pussy? Damn, what the hell was wrong with me?

Yet, if I didn't say something, she'd become suspicious and start asking all sorts of questions.

"Aight, put the phone up to his ear."

I could hear him softly breathing through the receiver.

"Go ahead, Cory."

I paused for a minute, trying to decide what to say. I didn't want to say nothing at all but then I thought about it, I had to say something. It may have been my last chance. I cleared my throat and tried to sound as normal as I could.

"Whud-dup playa... heard you got yo' eyes open and shit. It's a good thang too playa, cause nigga, some of yo' nurses got booty fo' days and thighs like what, ya heard me?"

I laughed, then I sat silent for a moment.

"Naw, seriously though man... I'm glad you aight. I don't know what I would do if something happened to you. Aey, guess whose crib I'm at? Aw shit, that was kinda dumb, huh? Anyways, I'm at that nigga Earl-the-Pearl's spot down in the hood. You should see this raggedy muthafucka."

My eyes began to water.

"Yeah... I had to come back to the place we grew up nigga and vibe on some shit. Look man, regardless of what... nigga I love you and I'm still down... like fo' flat tizes wit'cha playa. You feel me?"

"He heard you. His eyes are closed. Guess he's taking your words to heart. There's one more thing I've got to tell you. Hold on; let me move away from the bed. I don't want him to hear this and I don't know how to say it to you either."

It was bad news coming, I could tell by the tone in her voice.

"They're gonna do some tests in about an hour or so. The doctor did this outer limb test or something of the sort on him this morning and he can't feel his legs. The doctor..."

She began to cry.

"The doctor says he's probably paralyzed from the waist down."

That hit me like a ton of bricks. The fact that the shit was my fault fucked me up even worse and compounded the blow.

"Aey... aey Pooh, baby don't cry. My nigga is strong; he'll bounce back on top, one hundred percent. You gotta believe that shit. You can't accept nothin' less. You gotta be strong, especially around him. Cause if you low, he'll pick up on that shit. So, you gotta be positive so he'll draw strength from you. Aight? Aight baby?"

She sniffled.

"Alright, I'll try."

"Good, now relax. Get some rest and I'll call and check on you both in a few. I got some business to take care of first and then I'll stop through."

"Okay."

She blew me a kiss and told me that she loved me.

I closed up the phone and hung my head inside my hands.

Paralyzed?

I couldn't imagine my boy in no damn wheelchair for the rest of his life. Especially behind some shady shit with me and some trick. Speaking of... I wondered if she knew he was awake. I know she shit herself when she found out.

I flipped the phone open, dialed the number but when I hit the *send* button, her call was already coming in.

"You heard yet?" she asked.

She sounded like she'd just seen a ghost.

"Yeah, I heard. Pooh just hung up."

"So, what are we gonna do?"

"We? What the hell you mean, we? We ain't gon' do a muthafuckin' thang! You gon' stay the fuck away from me... 'memba?"

"Cory! You can not leave me in this boat to drown by myself... we..."

"The hell I can't! You betta get yo' ass a life jacket!"

"We're in this together, Cory."

"Hear me hoe, quit speankin' French! *We* ain't in a motherfuckin' thang," I spit out.

My rage towards her was growing deeper by the second.

"I knew I shouldn't have messed with yo' skank ass. My motherfuckin' boy layin' up there, paralyzed cause of us. What the fuck can we do? It's over now... the shit's about to hit the fan. He's up. What you want me to do?"

"You sorry son-of-a-bitch! I knew you wasn't shit. I don't know why I turned to you in my time of need. I don't why I messed with yo' sorry ass!"

"Well now... as I recall, you didn't think I was so sorry when you was swallowin' my soldiers," I chuckled.

"I'm glad you think it's so damn funny," she continued. "But what do you think Pooh will say when she finds out? You know what, it don't matter. All I need from you is a few pints of blood for our daughter, then you and the Jones' can all go to hell."

"Blood? What blood? I ain't givin' you no damn blood. You can cancel that shit."

"Cory, our daughter was born with antibodies to my blood, she needs a transfusion or she'll die. That's how Arman' found out she wasn't his. The blood, remember?"

She exhaled harshly.

"Look, all I'm asking you to do is save my baby, that's all."

"Man, I don't care about all that shit. I told yo' ass to get a damn abortion in the first place. I don't want no damn kids, especially by my best friend's skanchy ass wife."

"Well, he won't be your best friend for long, now will he? Look, you bring your hoe ass up here and give my baby what she needs to survive or I'll call Pooh and Momma Jones right now and tell them you're also the reason that Arman' is paralyzed. I'll tell them how he found out that you're AJ's father. Don't think I won't and don't think for a second, they won't believe me!"

Damn!

I hated that bitch more and more by the minute. Yet, I couldn't afford for her to tell the family shit. Couldn't let her charge me with a case like that.

"Yeah, aight. But after this, don't call me no muthafuckin' mo'. Bout no money, no diapers, no shit, you heard me? Cause I ain't givin' yo' ass nothin' else! And you bet not tell nobody I got yo' broke titty ass pregnant, caprende'? I ain't down fo' no daddy shit."

"Yeah, whatever. You just do what the fuck you suppose to do or else..."

I hung up the phone and lit up another spliff. I was getting to where I couldn't think straight without the shit. I exhaled a deep breath. I was totally pissed off. I couldn't believe that tramp had me by the balls and gave me a damn ultimatum. Fuck it, I had to do what I had to do.

Consequences of pussy gone bad.

I sat back, blazed up and thought about everything that could happen. It all made me nervous.

Ain't no way a broad gon' make me do a muthafuckin' thang. I got somethin' fo that ass.

I got up and went into the back room and woke up Earl. I told him to take a ride up to the hospital with me.

She wanna threaten a nigga? She think she got game like that? Shit, I got mo' game than Parker Brothers and Milton Bradley put together and I'm about to show her why...

Chapter Nine...Arman'

Slowly, I rolled my head to my left and focused in on the beautiful creature staring out the bay window of my room.

"Hello," I said.

My voice was both weak and raspy. The medication was easing the soreness in my throat and I was able to talk a little better. She spent around, smiled a smile that could light up the darkest room and rushed towards me.

"Arman' you're awake. Are you alright? Do you hurt anywhere? Do you need a doctor?"

"No," I said dryly. "But I would like some water though."

She held the pink plastic pitcher to my face and placed the straw inside my mouth so I could take a drink. The water felt good going down. I looked up at her and nodded my head to let her know I was done. She removed the straw and wiped the corners of my mouth with her fingers.

"Are you sure you don't need the doctor," she asked, watching my face wince in pain as I tried to reposition myself in the bed.

"I don't need a doctor but I would like to ask you a question."

Her smile faded and she possessed that same expression as earlier. She instantly tensed up. I cleared my throat again.

"What is your name?"

"Excuse me," she said.

"Your name, what is your name?"

She placed her hand on her hip.

"Arman', this is no time for joking. You know my name."

"No, I don't. As a matter of fact, I don't even know my own name. I hear you call me one thing and the little feisty, petite woman calls me something different. Look, really I need your help. I need you to tell me who I am and how I got here."

She slowly backed away from the bed, turned and said, "Hold on a second, I'll go get the doctor."

"I don't want a doctor dammitt! I want you to answer me."

She jumped and clutched her chest.

"Look, I'm sorry if I scared you but I'm not playing games here."

"You... you really don't know, do you?"

She began to cry. I waved her over to my bed side.

"Hey... hey, I said I was sorry. Don't cry. I just need you to tell what happened to me. Tell me who I am and who you are, please."

She wiped the tears from her face and sat down in the chair beside me. She really was a very beautiful woman. If she wasn't my wife or my girlfriend, maybe I should've been hit in the head.

"My name, my name is Terri," she began. "Terri Lambert. Your name," she cried.

"Your name is Arman'. Arman Letrey Jones. The little petite woman is your sister, Pooh. You have three but Pooh is the only one who lives here in Texas. The older woman, if you can remember her from earlier, is your mother Ozella but everyone calls her Momma J. You're here because you had an accident. A terrible accident the day before yesterday. Your concussion has apparently given you amnesia. You're a soldier in the Army, stationed here at Fort Hood. A very good one at that. You're married," she said softly.

"To you?"

She smiled and waved her hand.

"No, your wife's upstairs in the hospital as well."

"Why, was she in the accident also?"

"No, she just gave birth to a beautiful baby girl two days ago."

"So... I had an accident the day my baby was born?"

"Yes, can't you remember anything about that day? Where were you going? You were speeding so fast and hit a tree on a road you knew was dangerous. I don't understand where you could've been headed."

As she was talking, I clutched both my hands to my head because the painful picture reemerged. Only this time, it began to move slowly. Leaves... there were so many leaves. Lights were flashing and noises were blaring. Then it left again, along with the pain it caused.

"You alright, Arman'?"

She was standing to my side.

"Yeah, I'm fine. Please... continue."

She sat back down and readjusted herself in the chair.

"As I was saying. Your wife was down here last night to see you."

"A wife and a child huh?"

She looked away towards the window.

"And you," I asked. "What are you to me? You've been here the whole time. Even when I wasn't awake, I could feel you somehow. It's strange cause your voice, it was very soothing to me. Why? Why do I feel such a connection with you?"

She squirmed around, fidgeting with her fingers.

"I... I don't know. We're good friends."

"Friends?"

"Yeah, I'm in the Army also. Well, I was. I got out for a minute but I'll be going back soon."

"Really? Why you'd get out?"

"Uhh, my moms, yeah, my mother got sick. Anyway, I'm in Finance, you're in Infantry.

For what seemed like hours, she answered my questions. The nurse had come to administer my next dosage of medication and within minutes I was half asleep. I fought to keep my eyes open. I wanted to talk more. I had the strongest feeling she wasn't being totally honest with me on a few issues. Not about other things... about us.

Chapter Ten...Terri

I was so glad when he finally drifted off to sleep. I was afraid that if he kept asking me questions, he would begin to see right through me and know that I was hiding my feelings for him.

How could he not remember his life?

The doctor had warned us it was a possibility. He said that if it happened, hopefully it would only be temporary.

I went out to the nurse's station and alerted her of the news. Then I returned to the room and called Momma J and Pooh to tell them. Both were absolutely blown away. Momma J once again told me to pray and said she'd be up to the hospital soon. I promised her I would and hung up the phone.

I dialed Mrs. Carter to check on AJ and she told me he was taking a nap.

"That's good. Tell him that his mommy and daddy love him very much and I'll see him soon. Thanks… goodbye."

"You have a son?

He startled me.

"Oh, I thought you were sleeping. You scared me. Umm… yes, I have a son. He's fourteen months."

"What's his name?"

My heart did flip flops and I completely froze.

Was he playing tricks on me? Did he really have amnesia or was he leading up to his doubts about AJ, before the crash? Was he trying to get me to come out with it?

"His name is, umm... AJ."

"And what does AJ stand for?"

"Why do you ask," I responded a little defensively.

"I don't know, just making conversation, I guess. If we're so close, am I like his God-father or something?"

God father? More like father.

"Umm...no, you're more like, his uncle or something but now isn't the time to discuss all that. You need your rest."

"Maybe I'll see him soon?"

"I don't want the hospital scene to scare him or anything."

I felt as if I was about to throw up. My palms were soak and wet.

"You don't look so good, you alright?"he asked me.

"Uh-hum, just a little hungry, that's all."

Moments later, Alicia rolled into the room, followed by her nurse. Her mouth turned up the moment she saw me. I knew she was about to say something crazy. I put up my hand to stop her.

"Arman, your wife Alicia is here to see you."

He turned to me, sorta suddle and said, "Okay."

I rushed over to Alicia to shut her up before she had the chance to say something ignorant, again.

"Look Alicia," I said, placing my finger to my mouth. "He has amnesia. He doesn't remember anything, including you."

"What?" she whispered. "Amnesia?"

"Yes. I've told him about you and the baby though."

"Yeah well, did you tell him about the baby you tried to pin on him?"

My eyes began to burn, holding back the anger I felt inside for her.

Who does this bitch really think she is? I swear, if I didn't love Arman' so much, I'd see to it that bitch ended up on a milk carton. I mean, yeah, she had a right to not like me but to constantly throw darts at me is getting on my fucking nerves. God, I wanna break this ho's neck.

Instead, I simply answered, "No, I didn't tell him anything about me, AJ, or *our* family."

With that, I turned to leave but Arman' called after me.

"Aey, Terri?"

I turned to him.

"Yes?"

"Thanks for answering my questions and thank you for sitting here with me. Tell your son hello for me and if you're not to busy, can you come back tomorrow?"

She snickered as I passed her. I turned, smiled back at him and then looked back to Alicia.

"You're welcome and yes, I'll come back tomorrow."

I walked out door and gently closed it behind me. While in the parking lot, walking to my car, I could only imagine what she was telling him to turn him against me.

God, how I despised that woman.

As I drove down the garage ramp, I passed Cory and some guy, driving in. I blew the horn and kept going. I was too pissed off to deal with his arrogant ass.

I turned on the radio and the sounds of Music's *Love* took me back to Momma J's house and some sanity.

"… Love, ever since the first moment I spoke yo' name, from then on I knew, that by you being in my life, things were destined to change…"

I thought back to the moment I first realized I loved Arman'. It was the first night we'd made love. Yeah, It was only our first date, but when it's right, it's right. The way my soul set a fire when he looked at me with his bedroom eyes. The way the hair stood up on the back of my neck when he whispered in my ear. The tingle my body felt when he touched me. I knew he was the one… he would always be the one.

I still would do anything in the world for him. That included telling him that we meant nothing to each other until he was strong enough to deal with all the madness.

Amnesia is very unpredictable and there was no need to bring him any undo stress or harm. I'd do anything in my power to help him get better, knowing that, I'd still have to one day face up to all his accusations concerning AJ. However, until then, I'd pretend we meant nothing to each other... knowing in my heart, that was the furthest thing from the truth.

Chapter Eleven...Arman'

"... I just wanna know your name and maybe sometime we can hook up, hang out, just chill..."

The pretty brown skinned woman came over to my bedside dressed in a hospital gown. She looked exquisite. Her long, silky hair was pulled back into a clip.

"Hello sweetheart. I'm so glad you're finally awake. It's been a tough two days."

She grabbed me by my hand.

"So I hear," I whispered.

We shared an awkward moment of silence.

"How you feel?' she asked me.

"I'm aight, other than the fact that I don't remember nothin'."

"It's okay baby, it'll get better."

I sighed.

"So, tell me a lil bit about yo' self and our life together. I'm really sorry I can't remember anything but from the looks of things, I did alright, huh? I mean you... and a baby?"

She smiled. She had a beautiful smile. You couldn't tell me she had delivered a baby two days earlier outside of the fact that she was glowing and wearing a hospital gown.

"What do you want to know?"

"Well, we can start with how we met."

Her eyes began to sparkle.

"Well, I work at the Exchange on Post. That's where we live, on the base. I was working there when we met. You came in a lot, flirted with me back and forth until you finally got up enough courage to ask me out on a date."

"Oh yeah? Where we go?"

"To this club on Post called the NCO Club. It was love at first dance for us."

We both chuckled.

"We spent all out time together. We were inseparable. You had eyes only for me."

"I can see why," I said, smiling.

"Well, it took you so long to ask me out because you thought I was going to get with yo' best friend, Cory?"

"Cory?"

"Yeah, you guys have been friends since Pre-K. I'm sure he'll be in later to see you. You guys grew up together, joined the Army together and everything. He was your best man at our wedding."

"Sounds like he's my dog aight."

"Dog is the perfect word cause he's a hoe! Uses women like dish rags and throws them away. But thank God, you're nothing like him."

She stared off into space briefly before she began to tell me about the magical night, I proposed to her. The concert, the dinner, the hotel and everything.

I lay there thinking, *I'm a pretty smooth guy… and a lucky one too.*

It all sounded wonderful, she looked wonderful. I could sense that she loved me. Yet, for some reason, I didn't feel that connection, however beautiful she was, like I felt with Terri.

"You know Terri?"

"All to well."

"That didn't sound too good, what's up with that?"

"She's not a very real person. She pretends to be someone she's not. She's supposed to be your friend but on many occasions she's tried to disrupt our marriage. She slept with Cory and still tried to throw it at you on the d-l."

"Fo' real? That's funny, she don't seem like that type of person."

"My point exactly… she ain't what she seems."

The room grew quiet for a short time as I tried to take in what she'd said concerning Terri. Why did I care so much about her being near me? Why did what Alicia just say about her bother me so much? Had we had an affair? Is that why I felt so close to her? Couldn't have… I'm sure she would have told me earlier. Especially if she was out to destroy my marriage. I mean, why hide it? I made a mental note to ask her about it my next opportunity.

"Don't you wanna know about the baby," she asked.

"My bad, I'm sorry. Of course I do. What's her name?"

"Armanni, Armanni LaNee Jones. She was born uhh… a little premature and she's a little sick."

"What's wrong with her?"

"She contracted a blood disease from me that causes her own white cells to make antibodies to her blood but don't worry. She should be getting her transfusion from the blood they took from you after the accident shortly. Then she'll be as healthy as a bee. Once she's doing a little better, I'll se if they'll bring her down to see you, okay?"

"Aight… that would be nice. I'd love to meet my daughter. Ummm, Terri said something about me speeding in a rage somewhere down a dangerous street when I had my accident. Do you know where I was going and why I was so upset? I mean, she said it was the same day that the baby was born, so I can't understand why I would be so upset?"

Her face tensed and she became uneasy.

"See, that's what I'm talking about. I'm so sick of her assuming she can just tell you things that are my place to talk to you about. I don't think you were upset at all. I think you were speeding to tell Cory the good news about the baby, or maybe even to tell him about the difficulties of her birth, that's all."

"Probably," I resigned.

"So how long will you have to wait before your results come back on the tests on your spine?"

"The doc said a couple of hours."

"I'll come back then and let you get some rest. I have to go and check on the baby."

"Cool. I'll call up there later and talk to you… if that's okay with you."

She smiled that dazzling smile again.

"Of course it's aight with me silly. I'm your wife. I'll be waiting."

She gripped the chair to brace herself and slowly rose to her feet. She leaned down and placed a kiss on my lips. Her lips felt so soft and sweet.

"I love you baby," she whispered.

I felt bad because I didn't know how to respond.

"I'll call you," was all I could say.

As she rolled out the room I thought about Terri. I sensed a mystery there, especially with the way Alicia responded to the questions about her. I wished like hell I could remember a number for her. I wanted to talk to her again. But since I couldn't, I'd just have to lay there and dream of her as I drifted off to sleep.

She always tries to throw herself on you the d-l.

Shit, if she ever came onto me and I turned her down, I needed to flip over a few times in my car. Yet according, to Alicia, she was my best friend's girl and that's probably why I didn't get with her. Alicia said I only had eyes for her and that to me was just a typical female reply. Cause for the life of me, I couldn't see my eyes not wandering… especially at Terri.

Chapter Twelve...Cory

"...doin' what you gotta do is hard on the block sometimes. The game of life often comes down to a nickel or a dime..."

As Earl and I entered the parking lot, we passed by Terri. We exchanged waves. Good, I didn't need her ass asking me no more damn questions like she had the night before.

"Aey man, who was that," Earl asked.

"That's dat nigga Arman's baby momma. Dat's who he wanted all along, his ass was just caught up wit' dis trick up here. She love that nigga too man, mo' than life," I chuckled to myself. "Yeah, that's Queen B there."

"Shit, I know she fine as hell," he said.

That pissed me off.

How this ugly ass nigga got the nerve to call somebody fine, especially my boy's gal, looking like he been chewin' concrete?

"Nigga, shut yo' dumb ass up and get out the damn car. That's my boy's gal. Keep yo' perverted ass thoughts to yo' damn self."

"Shit, how you gon' act? I ain't the one that fucked his wife, you was."

I stopped in mid-stride and in one swift move, caught that nigga in his throat.

"Bitch ass nigga, don't you ever let that shit come outta yo' mouth again. I know what the fuck I did and I'm already caught the fuck up. Aey, don't catch the ass end of all this shit!"

He held his hands up in the air.

"Aight... aight dog, chill. I was just fuckin' wit' you nigga."

As we stood at the front of the entrance of Irwin Army, I laced up another joint. I was debating whether or not; I should go through with my plan. I couldn't afford no dumb shit from Alicia and I had to teach her ass a lesson.

Fuck it! I reasoned.

I had come too far to turn back now.

We went up to the third floor and I gave Earl my military ID card and let him give the blood for me. I had him dressed in a set of my BDU's. For me, going through with this was my only option. That bitch wouldn't let this end. She'd be at me the rest of my life. She'd never give me any peace. So I had to do what I had to do.

Plus, this gave me the ups on her with the family. If she didn't get no matching tests results, it was my word against her word and given the situation, my boy would believe me, off top.

When Earl came out of the lab, he shook his head at me.

"Man, you one cold muthafucka."

I pulled out two-one hundred dollar bills and handed it to him.

"Yeah nigga, whatever. I bet that warmed yo' ass right up!"

He began to smile and it showed his crooked, decayed teeth.

"No doubt my man... real warm."

Damn dope head.

"Come on nigga, I gotta go see my boy."

We went up to the ICU and headed for Arman's room. I told Earl to wait outside because I didn't know what awaited me on the other side of the door.

When I entered the room, he was lying there, eyes closed, looking so peaceful. I strolled over to his bed and took a seat. I began to talk to him, even though he was knocked out.

"Whad-dup playa? You lookin' good. Betta than the last time I saw you. I would've been up here sooner but I had some errands to run. I'll try to shoot through tomorrow after work. You know how it is with BC. He don't care if you blind, cripple or crazy... just have yo' ass at work on time!

He send's his well wishes and prayers though. Says he'll be up to see you later. Plus, you know we got range qualifications coming up. Shit nigga... I can't imagine the Army without you playa. This shit just ain't fair. I don't know why fucked up shit like this don't happen to nigga's who ain't got no future like that dumb ass nigga Earl.

I was gon' let him come in but looking at his ugly ass might send you back into the outer world," I chuckled.

"Damn, is he dat ugly?" Arman' said, half dazed.

"Hell yeah nigga, act like you don't know."

"I don't."

"Nigga quit bullshittin', that nigga just as ugly as his ass was when we was comin' up."

"You must be Cory."

"Nigga, you know there's only one nigga like me."

He extended his hand and I let mine drop inside.

"They didn't tell you? I got a concussion and I can't remember anything about my life before the crash."

I hung my head in shame. He had no idea how bad I felt for what I'd done.

"Uhh… Alicia, my wife, was down here earlier and she told me about you."

I can imagine!

I know he noticed the grimace on my face when he mentioned her name.

Damn, I couldn't stand that trick. Ain't no tellin' what she told him. Damn… Amnesia? He can remember nothin'? His mind and his body fucked up… damn!

"Damn dawg, I don't know what to say."

He looked at me.

"Cory, do you have any idea why I was speeding that day? Where was I going?"

"Naw man… I don't. But I live in the barracks over there. Nine times outta ten, you were headed to tell me something you felt was important. But aey… don't sweat all that. I'm a get you up and outta this bed and back on yo' feet in no time. And I'll fill you in on all I know, including our history while we do it, cool?"

"I'm wit' that."

He squeezed my hand.

It was a relief I still had him in my life for now.

"Aey… you know we down…"

I waited for our mutual ending. I felt crushed when I realized he couldn't finish the sentence. How could he? He couldn't remember its ending.

"It's all good playa, I got 'cha," I told him.

Pooh and Momma J walked in.

"Hey baby," Pooh said walking over to me.

I stood up to receive her in my arms.

"Hey baby girl, whad-dup wit' it?"

I placed a juicy kiss on her lips.

"Boo, why you smell like smoke?"

"Shit, a nigga been stressed the fuck out. It's nothin' fo' you to worry about though."

She looked at me scornfully and I quickly shifted her focus.

"Aey… look who's up."

Her face beamed.

"Manni, you're awake."

"Yeah, I guess I am."

"How's my baby boy this afta'noon," Momma J asked.

"I guess I'm aight, I mean, given the circumstances."

"Aww son, dis here is just God's way of preparin' you fo' somethin' down the road. One thang 'bout God... He don't make no mistakes, hear?"

"Yes ma'am. So, I've been told I've got three sisters total. I know you're one of 'em and the other two live out of state or somethin' like that, right?"

"Yeah, Tonya's the oldest. She lives in Cali with her husband and Donna is overseas in the Navy. They call to check on you all the time. Matter-of-fact, Donna just called about an hour ago. Ya'll are cool and everything but you and I were always the closest and..."

Pooh began to cry.

"Why you cryin'?" he asked.

"Cause you don't remember me."

I rose up behind Pooh and hugged her tightly, whispering in her ear.

"Memba what I told you, about him feelin' low if he sees us trippin'?"

She shook her head.

"Back up baby, he don't need to see you like this. Strength... he needs yo' strength."

"Ok," she said as I turned her into my chest.

92

"It's aight Pooh, I'm gon' be fine. My boy here says he gon' help me get outta this bed and back on my feet and then I'm sure in no time, my memory will come back."

I think he was trying to re-assure himself more so than us.

"Dat's right son. You's gotta have faith in this here thang," Momma J said, smiling.

"We just left dat beautiful baby girl of yo's. I tell you she must look just like her momma's folks cause I don't see none of you in 'er nowhere."

Imagine that, I mumbled to myself.

"Yeah? Alicia told me earlier that she was gonna see if they would bring her down as soon as they transfused her with my blood today because she was a little sick."

What?

I almost passed out.

That dirty bitch!

She tried to use me in order to save that baby so she could keep her clutches in my boy.

Scandalous… bitches is so fuckin' scandalous! That's exactly why I treat them the way I do. Bitch, don't ever try to play a playa. Cause every time you play pussy, you gon' get fucked. That I promise you!

"Hey… you alright baby," Pooh asked.

"Yeah, I'm cool. I'm just wonderin' if you wanna come over to the crib and chill fo' a minute later on. Get yo' mind off all this."

She smiled.

"And how do you suppose we do that?"

I laughed.

"Get yo' mind out the gutta girl! I just wanna chill."

"Aight, you right. We can hook up later."

She looked at her wrist that bore the gold Chanel watch Arman' had given her for her birthday a few months back.

"Around?" I asked, trying to maintain her focus.

Her eyes were starting to well up with tears again.

"Around seven?"

"Cool. I gotta drop my boy off and then I'll be waitin'."

I kissed her on the cheek.

I walked over to Momma J and leaned down to place a kiss on her forehead.

"Take care of 'em moms. Call me if you need anything. Anything, aight?"

"You always was my second son," she said, smiling.

"I always said God put the two of you togetha cause he knew Manni' needed a brotha and I couldn't have no mo' kids. I'm so glad he got you."

I looked over at my boy and smiled, thinking to myself.

No, I'm glad I still got him.

I looked back to her and smiled.

"Me too, moms."

I walked over to Arman' and gripped his hand.

"Aey… stay up playa. I'll be back tomorrow after work, aight?"

"Aight. Aey… how long you been kickin' it with my sista?"

I looked to Pooh and chuckled.

"Shit nigga, I been tryin' to hit that since I took my diaper off."

We laughed.

It felt good to hear him laugh again.

"But hell, she just gave in a little over a year ago. Tryin' to play all hard and shit."

"And Terri?"

"What about her?"

He looked confused.

"Didn't you…"

The doctor walked in and interrupted us. He was holding Arman's x-rays in his hand.

"Evening folks. I have the test results back for Mr. Jones and I thought you'd all like to hear them."

We all gave him our undivided attention.

"Well, the swelling around the spinal cord has subsided impressively and enough for us to x-ray the lower vertebrae. The damage to the spinal cord seems to be very minimal. Minimal in a sense that it's very probable you can walk again…"

"Hell yeah," I screamed.

"Thank you Lawd," Momma J followed.

"You's always on time."

"Let me finish," he said, holding his hand in the air.

"A lot will depend on physical therapy and you. Your will and determination will provide the outcome. We'll start you next week daily exercises and try to sit you up and see how it goes, okay?"

"Aight, thanks doc."

"You're welcome soldier."

That word brought a smile to his face.

"Ummm… excuse me doctor. Ummm… what about his memory? How long will he be like that?" I asked.

"Hard to say. Truth is, some people never regain theirs back."

He walked out the door and I looked over at my boy.

How could I have done this to him?

The only way I could make it up to him I felt, was to get him well. That beyond a shadow of a doubt, I'd do.

Chapter Thirteen...Cory

"... I don't see nothin' wrong, with a little bump and grind..."

I dropped off Earl and headed over to Panda Express for some Chinese take out. I picked up my favorite Chow Mein noodles and Orange Chicken. I swung by the Class Six and picked me up a case of MGD's and a pint of Hennessey.

Driving along, I thought about how much I admired Arman'. His ability to sacrifice himself, to love and commit. I'd never possessed those qualities within myself. Thanks to my daddy, women were always a game to be played whenever I wanted. A game I had to win at all costs.

I could never let a woman get to me or get over on me. Hell, I couldn't even spell whipped. Deep inside, I think I despised them for breaking up my family. That's why I dogged them like I did. I was never giving any of them a chance to get close to me or hurt me again.

None, except for Pooh. It had been a year and I was still kicking with her. Not monogamously of course. I mean I still hit skins on the side but it was a start. Hell, a year was already twelve months past my normal schedule.

And although I'd stepped out on her with other women, they didn't mean nothing to me. They were just something to occupy my time and prove to myself that I could still hit whatever, whenever I wanted, including Alicia.

I was really feeling Pooh though; maybe even enough to chill with just her some day.

Nawww, who the hell am I kiddin'.

Ain't no way, no woman was putting me on lock down. Variety's the spice of life and I'm a nigga that loves spices!

I cleaned up the crib and sprayed a little Fahrenheit cologne all around. A few weeks ago, I'd brought this plug in fireplace that was supposed to set the mood in any weather and I'd been waiting to try it out.

I cut the lights down, hit the switch and it came to life. The real life animation of the logs crackling made the mood official.

Oh yeah… flossy.

I cruised to the stereo and chose my selection of smooth grooves for the night. Luther, Freddie, Patti, Force MD's and Genuine were all there. Teddy P was my head liner.

Seven sharp, she was at my door. She'd been home to change and stepped inside wearing a knockout sundress, showing off all the curves.

"Damn baby, that dress is definitely wearin' you!"

"You mean, I'm wearin' it, don't you?"

I wrapped my arms around her from the back and squeezed her waist.

"Hell naw… the way it's clingin' to them curves, it's definitely wearin' you."

"Cory, you're such a dog," she said, turning to me.

"Bow wow, baby," I responded, kissing her.

I drove my tongue inside her mouth and my hands up under that dress. The spliff I'd smoked on the way home had me hornier than a bitch in heat.

"Damn boo, what happened to just chillin'?"

"You knew when you walked in here with that muthafuckin' dress on that chillin' was out the window. But we can chill… after I get this ass."

I smiled.

I tongued her down as I backed her up to the bed. I picked up the remote, hit the stereo and shut down the lights.

"Nice touch," she said, nodding at the fire place.

"Oh yeah, I thought about this body glowing in the flames when I bought it."

"Oh Cory, you so silly."

"I'm so serious."

I lifted the sundress over her head and tossed it over to the couch. She knew exactly what she'd come for. Her bra-less chest and black laced thong told me so. As I traced her body with my hands, Teddy P laid the ground work.

"… *ummm, it used to be, every night I would cry my heart out, over you. It remind me of when you and I were so much in love. I couldn't eat, couldn't sleep, I'd just sit at home and I'd weep but now all that changed, I've found someone to ease my pain. And it don't hurt now, no not now...*"

Her pussy was spilling juices onto my hand before I even entered her. Teddy and I always had that effect on women. Pooh hadn't been around that much. I could tell that by her pussy's ability to only handle two fingers at a time. It was always such a struggle to get inside her and my dick hung; I know a good eight inches on hard.

I thrust my fingers inside her, loving the way she made her body grind on my hand.

"You miss daddy?"

"You know it," she panted and replied.

"How bad? Show me how bad you missed daddy."

She dropped to her knees, reached over to the candy dish on the table and placed her favorite Fire flavored jolly rancher in her mouth.

"Oh yeah, you gon' suck daddy's dick real good tonight huh?"

"Don't I always?" she asked as she placed my jimmy inside her mouth. The logic of the jolly rancher was that it made the walls of her mouth hotter which in turn made the pleasure of the experience double.

She slowly slid her lips down my jimmy and eased back up to the top. When she came up, she inhaled deeply yet softly and brought a breath of cool air with her across my jimmy.

"That's right baby... take it to 'em."

By that, she knew I meant to deep throat it.

She obeyed my command as she pulled me all the way back to her tonsils and massaged the sensitive vein at the center of my jimmy with her tongue ring. Damn, the stress we both had been under made this shit off the hook.

"Do what I like."

She left my jimmy and ran her tongue down to my balls. She placed them inside her mouth and began to hum, causing them to vibrate and drive me crazy Then she took my jimmy, began rubbing and slapping it all across her face. I loved to see that shit. All over they eyes, they noses and their mouths.

"You ready? Huh? You ready to feel this dick?"

"Yes, I'm ready."

"Get up."

She stood up and I grabbed her arms as hard as I could and slammed her up against the wall with her back to me.

"Don't hurt me," she pleaded.

"Shut up bitch and take this dick like a woman."

I wrapped the belt to my bathrobe around her hands and a scarf around her mouth. She could neither move nor scream. Bondage... I loved bondage.

As I fiddled with her pussy lips, I began to talk to her.

"Check it out... you at the club. Lookin' fine as a muthafucka and I'm tryin' to holla but you won't give a nigga no play. I sit back in the cut and wait fo' you to leave the club..."

I wiggled my way inside her. She was drenched. Her pussy wrapped so snugly around my jimmy.

"… When I see you leavin' the club, I get up and follow you outside. I walk slowly behind you so you're unaware of my presence. I sneak up behind you. I grab you from the back and cover yo' mouth. You're scared; I love the fear in you…"

She was squirming about frantically as I long dicked her from the back. Her back arched and her legs began to shake. She loved to role play as much as I did.

"… I tell you to shut up. Don't make a sound. You know what I want and I'm a get it. I rip yo' panties from yo' body and bend you over the hood of the car…"

I pulled her away from the wall and turned her towards the nightstand. She bent over and held on as best she could as I thrust inside her deeper and deeper. The more she attempted to scream, the harder I hit it.

"…I plunge inside you. Grippin' yo' hair from the back so I could see yo' face. See that you liked it as much as I did. Your pussy answers fo' me as yo' juices flow onto my dick…"

I could feel the bottom of her womb slamming against the head of my jimmy. The pussy was popping the loud fart noises I loved so much.

"Yeah baby, make it talk to me, make my pussy cat meow."

She wiggled her way out of the belt and untied her mouth. She let go of the nightstand and bent down to grab her ankles. I was taxing it freely with nothing blocking the path to my destination.

I reached up under her and stroked her pearl tongue.

"… I want that ass. You try to resist me but I'm taking it anyway. You try to scream for help. I slap that ass hard and forceful. You're cryin' now, upset at yo'self because you lovin' it. Pissed off because you nuttin' all over my dick."

Her body began to spasm as I thrust my thumb inside the pink opening between her ass cheeks. She was a feind for both holes being occupied at the same time. Simultaneously, both her ass and her pussy let off, drenching my balls and thighs with cum.

"Hell yeah… that's what I'm talkin' bout baby, drop it all… let it rain down on me… uuummm, daddy's bout to cum baby… you know what I want… uuuhhhh, you know what I need… get it… come and get it."

She spun around and like a leach, gripped my jimmy in her mouth and my sacks released bullets into her throat. She pulled back to let some squirt all over her face, just like I liked it. She always pleased me, never lackin'. That's probably why I've been with her so long and never intended to let her go. I felt justified in doing what I did with Earl cause I had to protect mines, by any means necessary.

I went into the bathroom to get her a towel. I lit up another spliff. Then I drank the concoction Earl gave me to drop the Cain from my system. I brushed my teeth and went back in the room to continue handling my business with my baby.

   She was ready and waiting for round two. I closed my eyes and imagined for a moment this could possibly last forever. And it could… as long as Alicia kept her fuckin' mouth shut!

Chapter Fourteen...Arman'

"...dream if you will a picture, of you and I engaged in a kiss. The sweat of yo' body covers me. Can you my darlin', can you picture this..."

I had been here, from my knowledge, over a week now and my legs were getting stronger everyday. The family had been so supportive, especially Cory and Terri. They all had alternated time with me but it was something about those two.

I had become closer to my wife, truth-be-told but I didn't feel anything close to what I felt for Terri. I dreamed of her almost every night. I thought of her most of the day. I thought about Alicia too and I tried to reject the thoughts of Terri in my head but they were just that strong.

I felt wrong for that in a way because I was married and Alicia seem to really love me. She called me every night and came to visit as often as she could cause she spent most of her time with our baby. I was supposed to meet my daughter for the first time later that evening.

I was so excited about that. I had heard from the family how beautiful she was. I knew somewhere deep inside of me that I must've loved my wife deeply at one point. But Terri was like a drug to me and I was slowly, with each passing day, becoming more and more addicted to her.

I was lying there, waiting on the nurse to give me my daily

sponge bath. I was scheduled for therapy later that day with Cory. While contemplating all the hard work I was about to endure, the door came open and in walked a goddess. Looking as gorgeous as always, dressed in a thin, curve fitting dress.

"Hey there, good to see you up. I thought you'd still be resting."

"Naw, I've been up fo' a while now. Just doin' some thinkin'... bout you."

She looked surprised.

"Me?"

"Yeah, you... there's somethin' I'd like to ask you."

Again, she tensed up, automatically. I didn't understand that. I mean, what could I possibly ask her to make her so jumpy and scared.

"Ask me something, about what?"

"About you."

"What about me?"

"Well first off, why don't you come and chill in the chair next to me. I won't bite you."

She rested in the chair beside my bed. I took a moment to admire every perfect feature of her face.

"So, what do you wanna know?"

"My wife told me something a while back that was very intriguing to me."

"Really and what was that?" she asked with a curious look.

"Well, she told me that you and my boy Cory used to kick it and…"

"What?"

I held my hands up in the air to calm her down.

"I'm sorry, go ahead."

"She said you guys use to kick it and I'm just tryin' to figure out what happened cause I see him kickin' it now with my lil sister. I mean what, were you his woman on the side or somethin'? I'm only askin' cause she also told me that you use to… you know, try to get at me, on the low. Is that true? I mean, she portrayed you like some lil groupie or somethin' and I just don't see that in you."

She massaged her temples and it was clear something was very wrong between the two of them cause her blood was literally boiling through her skin. Then she stood up and began walking towards the window.

"I don't know what to say… I mean… I'm blown away."

"Blown away? You mean you pissed… It's written all over your face. You upset cause she told me or because it's not true? I mean you don't have to think of what to say… say the truth."

"Who's version?"

"Yours."

She returned to her seat, crossed her legs and exhaled.

"Arman'… I've always respected your marriage and your wife. I've never done anything to break up your home. Sometimes women just can't handle their husbands being as close to another woman as you and I was."

"We must've been awful close, cause you're definitely not one of her favorite people."

She laughed and I enjoyed the ora her smile brought to the room.

"We were that tight, huh?" I asked.

"Skin tight," she said with a slight chuckle.

"And as for yo' boy Cory, I won't even go there."

It got quiet for a minute.

"I went upstairs to see your baby girl, I hope you don't mind."

"Why would I mind? How... uuuuuuhhhh..."

A pain shot through my head, along with the moving images again. Policeman, fireman... moving me. Lights, lots of lights continued to flash.

"Arman', are you alright? Arman'?"

I gripped my head tightly and waited for the pain to subside.

"I'm okay," I told her.

She placed her hand on top of mine.

"Yeah, I just get these flashes of images that pop into my head sometimes."

"What kind of images? What do they look like?"

"Leaves at first, then came the sirens... now I can see the

police and firemen."

"Maybe you're remembering' the crash. I mean, that's what it sounds like to me."

"I don't know, maybe you right."

I smiled at her and she smiled in returned. Our eyes locked into a deep gaze until she looked away.

"Well, I'm starting my real therapy today. The doctor says my legs are strong enough to handle it now. I'm headed down there in a few hours when Cory gets here."

From out of nowhere, she sprang up and slammed a big juicy kiss on my lips.

"What was that about?" I asked her, wiping my mouth.

"I know right, I'm so sorry, I shouldn't have done that. I'm just so happy you're alright. Please forgive me."

"Forgive you? Fo' what, fo' havin' some soft ass lips."

She smiled.

The young, perky white nurse entered the room with all my sponge bath accessories in her hands.

"Mr. Jones, are you ready fo' your sponge bath?"

She was too hyper and shit. She looked all too eager to be playing with my nuts. So I looked over at Terri and smiled. I had a better idea.

"Uh, Terri?"

She turned quickly to pick up her keys and her purse.

"I'm sorry. I'll be back later."

I reached for her.

"No, no; I don't want you to come back later."

She looked at me bewildered and asked, "You don't?"

"No, I didn't mean it like that. I was wondering… if you'll stay and you know help me with my sponge bath."

A blush came over her hot enough to melt the biggest iceberg.

"You want me to help bathe you?"

"Unless you feel uncomfortable, then it's okay. I mean, I know I'm married and all. But if we cool, it ain't about all that, right? Personally, I'd just rather have someone I feel close to, to wash my private parts. But I mean… if you can't handle it…"

She threw her purse down in the chair and put her hand on her hip.

"I can handle it, I ain't scared."

She took the accessories from the nurse, thanked her and excused her. Terri went into the bathroom and filled the pail with hot soapy water. She laid out all the things she would need on the tray beside her.

I removed my arms from my gown, exposing the upper part of my chest. She began washing my face, my neck and went down to my chest. Every touch was so tender and her hands felt so good. She brought alive what few working nerves I had left. She washed my arms and my hands.

She sat down on the side of the bed and pulled me towards

her so she could wash my back.

"You do this well," I told her.

"Glad you like it."

Our faces were inches apart and again, we locked into a gaze that could only be described as need. I needed to know what was between us and why I felt this way about her. She needed to stay in control to keep the distance she pretended we had between us.

She leaned into me but caught herself.

"Umm... let's dry off your back so I can lay you back down."

She dried my back and helped me to lie back. She removed the sheet across my lap. She dipped the rag and stopped. She looked into my eyes as she softly began washing my inner thighs.

"Can you feel this?"

I shook my head.

"No."

I sure as hell wished I could.

She went all the way down to my feet before coming up to wash between my legs. She re-dipped the rag, reached for my jimmy and said, "Arman' are you sure I should be doing this? I mean, wouldn't you rather have your wife do it?"

I looked at her, took my hand and covered hers on my thigh.

"No. Number one, she can't. Number two, I asked you."

I took her hand and placed it on my jimmy.

"Don't be afraid."

She sat back down on the side of the bed and stared into my eyes as if she were afraid to look down.

As she washed me, I felt a tingling sensation that began in my left nut sack.

She dipped the rag again and began washing. The tingling was still there.

"Terri, kiss me."

"Huh?"

I pulled her to me and softly began to kiss her. She opened up to receive me and God, it was like heaven. She began to massage the rag more firmly than before. I could feel the rag's roughness. She could feel me getting semi' hard. She sprung up in surprise.

"Arman'... baby, it's... getting... hard... it's getting hard!"

"I know... but before we tell the doctor... take yo' shoes off."

She looked into my eyes and knew exactly what I wanted.

"Look, I don't care if you've been with my best friend... hell, I can't even remember my best friend fo' real. But there's somethin' between us, somethin' very deep and I'm sorry. I know I'm married but I can't help the way I feel about you and I can't stop thinkin' about you no matter hard I try. I felt you... I wanna feel you. There's just some..."

She rushed my mouth and devoured me so, it left me breathless.

She removed her shoes, climbed on the bed with me but hesitated to move any further. She wanted to make sure that it was safe for me.

"Can you do this?"

I looked at her, smiled and said, "Watch me... better yet, feel me."

I moved her panties to the side and she guided me in. I feel you Terri."

"I feel you too baby."

"No, I really feel you. Your heat, your walls... don't stop baby. I feel you."

I grabbed her breast and pulled them to my face, circling each nipple before gently biting them.

She moaned out in pleasure.

"Ohhh baby, that feels so good. I've missed you so much."

I knew it. We'd been here before.

"I know you missed me Terri, I could see it in yo' eyes. Eyes never lie. Look at me..."

She looked into my eyes.

"Look deeply... do you see somethin', anything? Anything familiar?"

"Yes... I do... love."

"Hold on to that Terri. I want you to hold on to that. I need you to hold onto me."

I gripped her ass and she arched her back, allowing me to go deeper inside her.

"Damn Terri, is it always like this?"

"Always."

With every turn of her body, she generated more and more feeling back into my body. She had been the medicine I needed all along. I loved the feel of her. She loved the feel of me.

She dug her nails in my waist as she worked her pelvic bone beyond anything I could ever imagine. She was the bomb. I felt her about to explode, her g-spot swelling against the head of my jimmy.

She pulled me close to her and panted in my ear. Tears flowing down her face.

"No one has ever loved you like I do... no one ever will."

With that she came, long and hard, followed by me. The explosion sent chills throughout my body. She collapsed on top of me, crying her soul out.

"Terri," I said, gently stroking her hair.

"Please tell me why you're crying."

"You're married Arman', and no matter how much is between us, I can't have you. You have a family that needs you very much. And I've always tried to respect that. I've always loved you with a passion I can't begin to explain. I've loved you enough to let you go and be where you felt you needed to be."

I ran my fingers through her hair and placed a soft kiss on her forehead.

"Well, right now I can't remember where the hell that is. All I know right now, is that I've got somethin' very deep in my heart fo' you and you won't tell me why. You know what I think? I think we did have somethin' goin' on, somethin' so very deep and that's why this just happened. I feel you Terri... even when you're not around and I can't figure out why. Us fuckin' around is the only thing that makes sense to me."

She shifted her body and begun sliding her leg across me. She slid off the bed, stood up and began fixing her dress.

"Arman', we've known each other for a very long time. And I've said some things here today in a moment of passion that I shouldn't have said. Yes, we've had moments like this before but the bottom line is the same as it's always been, you're married boo and that takes precedence over anything else."

I turned away from her as she washed her scent and her juices from my body. She wasn't telling me the truth; I felt it in my heart. Yet, my mind told me maybe she was. Maybe Alicia was right... maybe she was just a groupie.

"Aight, have it yo' way," I told her.

"Look baby, I love you. That's no secret. Even your family and your wife knows that but you're mar..."

"Why do you keep sayin' that? You know I'm married, I know I'm married. But being married didn't just stop us from fuckin' now did it?"

I was getting a little pissed off.

"No, it didn't and I…"

Her eyes welled up with tears again and felt bad for raising my voice with her.

"I shouldn't have taken advantage of you in this… in your situation."

"Come here, Terri."

She sat down beside me and leaned against my chest.

"You didn't do anything of the sort. Terri you just gave me back the feeling in my entire lower body. And if your lovin' has that type of power, then by all means, please… take advantage of me more often!"

She smiled then.

"Aey, look… we're both adults. Amnesia don't take away emotions, desires, lusts nor your ability to want, to need or be pleasured. I probably wanted you more than you wanted me. Who in their right mind wouldn't? From the moment my eyes opened, I had to have you. Don't feel guilty, please. I don't.

I feel as if you and I have a story to finish and no matter what you say, this is only the beginning."

Chapter Fifteen... Terri

"...It's been a long, a long time comin' but I know a change is gon' come, oh yes it will..."

There was just no way around it anymore. He could feel the love I had inside for him all along. In a way that warmed my heart but in another, it frightened me. To realize that once he got his memory back, he'd hate me again, was the scariest feeling I'd ever felt.

I'd just made love to him and even with his mind on vacation; his body still felt the same inside of mine. His rough touch still felt wonderful. His long stiff penis still penetrated every fiber of my being. I couldn't hide it any longer, he knew. What my mouth couldn't say, my body did.

As I walked out the bathroom fixing my hair, Arman' looked at me pointedly and asked, "So, you ready to tell me the truth about..."

Cory strolled in mid-sentence.

"Playa, playa... you ready to do this?"

He walked over and slapped five with Arman' and glanced over to me and said, "Aey, uh Terri, how you doin'?"

I waved.

"Ummm, I'm glad you here. Can I holla at you outside fo' a minute?"

I looked to him and then to Arman'. I agreed because I

figured he might have some new information about Arman's condition.

"Sure Cory. Umm, Arman', I'll be right back."

He rolled his head over to the side.

"Aey, right back playa," Cory said.

We went outside and as I stood beside him, arms folded, I braced myself for another insult.

"Aey... look Terri, I owe you an apology. Fo' a long time, I been givin' you the raw end of all this shit. I thought you weren't the right one fo' my boy but I was mistaken'. You the perfect one. I saw you the other day at the Class Six. You didn't know I was there, in the next line over from you. Anyways, some cat was tryin' to push up on you but you represented. You told 'em you had a man. I like that in you.

You've always had his back and I got mad respect fo' you fo' that. I mean, don't get me wrong, some shit you coulda done a lil different, you know, like runnin' off every time shit got deep but aey... we all do things without thinkin' sometimes. I just wanted you to know that... that nigga in there, he loves you, he always have."

The tears began to form in my eyes. It was so special to hear this coming from Cory. I never expected to hear one nice word from him, let alone his blessing for me and Arman' to be together.

"Thanks Cory, you really, really don't know how much that

means for me to hear you say that."

"Yeah well, it's rare to find a chick that's down fo' a nigga like you been. I can't do nothin' but respect that."

"No, it's not that hard. You just gotta slow down long enough to recognize her when she comes. Matter-of-fact, I believe she already has, don't you?"

He smiled as I playfully hit him on the arm.

"Yeah, you might be right. I don't know... but in any event, I'm glad you got my nigga's back."

He checked his watch.

"Well, I gotta get this nigga down to therapy so we can get started on gettin' his legs back in shape."

"Oh Cory, I'm sorry, I almost forgot to tell you the best news of the day. He got some feeling in his legs."

"Straight?" he asked as he hugged me.

We locked our arms around each other in the mutual love we both felt for Arman'.

"That's tight. How that happen?"

I felt a little embarrassed to answer.

"When I was giving him a sponge bath," I giggled.

"A sponge bath? You gave that nigga a sponge bath? No wonder he got some feelin' back in his shit. And what? The nigga got to excited?"

My look gave it away.

"Aw hell naw, that's a damn shame. Ya'll just nasty."

He shook his head.

"That's my boy, still rippin' it up, twisted nuts and all."

He began to laugh.

"Yeah. that's my nigga… playa, playyaaa."

I laughed.

"Hell, he might not need to go to therapy now. Shit you already gave his ass a workout. He probably ain't got no damn strength left."

We laughed as I pinched him on the arm.

"Come on."

When we entered the room, Arman was visibly upset. His face was tense and his lips were twisted up at the corners. I leaned in to give him a kiss goodbye. He answered with semi-puckered lips and a quick, dry smack.

"I've gotta go and get AJ but I'll be back first thing in the morning, Okay? Rest well."

His kiss felt cold for the first time in the years I've known him.

"Yeah, whatever."

I looked at him, puzzled at what he could be so upset about. Then I figured that maybe he wanted to know what me and Cory was talking about privately, especially since Alicia had told him we used to kick it. But time wouldn't allow me to get into that at that moment. It was late and I had to go.

As I closed the door behind me, I smiled to myself. It was

kind of cute to see him jealous. On the other hand, I wanted to choke Alicia for all the bullshit she had told him.

One day, I swear I'm gonna light into that bitch!

I couldn't stand her but maybe for all the wrong reasons. Mostly because every moment she spent with Arman' as his wife, was a moment I spent, wishing it was me.

Chapter Sixteen... Cory

"... got me down a down nigga on my team, the Bonnie and Clyde theme..."

The nurse and I helped Arman' into his wheelchair. He still had amazing strength in his upper body. The little perky, big bosomed white nurse seemed too over-joyed grabbing on his chest and upper arms.

"Oh, Mr. Jones, you have such nice muscles."

He smiled a reply and chuckled.

"Thanks."

I shook my head at the tramp, thinking how, in one breath, they hated our asses and in another breath, they always tryin' to get into nigga's pants.

We rolled him down to the elevator and then down to the second floor physical therapy room at the end of the hall. It was a private room equipt with all the machines we would need to get my boy back on his feet.

"You ready to do this, playa?" I asked as he scanned the room, intimidated by all the weight machines. I could sense his resistance. I rubbed his shoulders.

"Aey man, you can do this. You just gotta get into that same mentality you had in basic training."

I began to laugh thinking about how crazy we were together in basic training. I kneeled down beside him.

"Everyday, you use to tell me you was quittin'."

"Yeah, why was that?" he asked as I locked the wheels on his wheelchair, stood behind him, grabbed him around his waist and helped him down onto the floor mat. I grabbed his right ankle and began stretching his lower calf muscles.

"Man, basic training was hell for you. You didn't wanna be there anyway. You really only joined the army cause I didn't wanna go off and leave Dallas without my boy. You in pain?"

I lifted his right leg slowly in the air, slightly twisting it side to side as I raised it.

"Naw, not pain but it is a lil tense. Keep going though."

He exhaled a deep breath.

"So, you were sayin'? I joined the service cause you thought a nigga was gon' develop separation anxiety? Damn, we must've been hella tight for me to follow you into Uncle Sam's house."

He laughed.

"Man, we been so tight fo' so long, I couldn't imagine leaving my brotha behind. We had this drill Sergeant right…"

I started chuckling again.

"She used to stay on yo' ass all the time. Nigga, I personally think it was cause the lil bitch wanted to fuck you, you heard me?"

I slapped him on the hip. He laughed then.

"Word?"

He suddenly drifted off into his own little world so, I just continued to work his leg muscles. I simply let him be and gave him his own space. It had to be a fucked up feeling not to be able to remember your life. The people that mattered to you the most. I thought about all the things that would happen when he could remember.

All the explaining I would have to do. The lies, the betrayal and all the pain it had caused and would continue to cause for years to come.

All fo' some pussy.

All because I had allowed my ego to rule my mind and common sense. I'd cost my boy so much, too much. I'd gotten so lost in tripping off all that crazy shit, I didn't hear him call my name. He hit me on the arm.

"You good?" he asked.

"Yeah playa… I'm just glad you aight… you know?"

"I feel you. So now, back to us. We were closer than close, huh? Tight like glue?"

"Oh, hell yeah. Tighter than a fat bitch's girdle and closer than black folk's lips to a piece fried chicken!"

He fell back and burst into laughter. It felt good to see that. Even though his mind was different, Amnesia couldn't change the sound of his voice.

I began to push his left leg towards his chest. He complained of only minor pain.

"So Cory, help me out. I mean explain to me how you ended up with my sister. Why you stop fuckin' with 'ol girl?"

"Nigga, peep game. She finally recognized how flossy a nigga was at yo' weddin' and shit. She was fuckin' with some lame ass nigga Kevin who got some bitch pregnant on her. She dumped him and I got the digits on the rebound tip. Once a nigga got in, it was on. I quit fuckin' with Punkin shortly after that."

"My sista-n-law Punkin? Damn man, you use to hit her too?"

"Well, I just use to hit that hoe every now and then until somethin' better came along. And it did, so I got ghost. I mean Punkin was cool. She helped me get the engagement night and shit together fo' you and Alicia. I mean, she served her purpose and shit but when it was time to bounce, it was time to bounce."

He shook his head.

"Aight that's all good nigga but I ain't talkin' about her. I'm talkin' about Terri. Why you stop fuckin' with her? She's one bad ass…"

"Who?" I interrupted.

I know he ain't just say who I think he said.

"Terri? Yo' baby momma, Terri? Who the hell told you I was fuckin' yo' baby momma?"

"My baby what? Baby momma? Naw, man… Terri…"

"Nigga, yo' baby momma!"

He looked so confused. How could he not have known? I was sure one of them told him who she was. I mean, who did he think she was, hangin' around all this time.

Wasn't they fuckin' less than thirty minutes ago?

"I ain't followin', too many names up in the air. I'm confused. Alicia told me you use to fuck with Terri, right or wrong?"

Only Alicia could have come up with some twisted shit like that to poison his mind against Terri. I bit my bottom lip to refrain from disrespecting the tramp in front of him but she was getting to buck with it.

Damn, is she that fuckin' desperate? That hoe got some major issues, tellin' him some shit like that. No wonder he seemed pissed when Terri and I left the room together.

"Dawg, I would never hit yo' baby momma. That damn girl worships the ground you…"

He held his hand up to catch my attention.

"Wait, wait, wait... so Terri really do have a baby by me?"

"Ummm, never mind all that. You…uh… talkin' bout… uh…"

I was speechless.

He closed his eyes and clinched his fist. He was mumbling more to himself than me.

127

"Why they lie to me? Both of 'em. Baby momma?"

I lifted him up on the bench so he could begin lifting weights. We began small, using only ten pound weights. I felt bad because deep inside, I knew the reason Terri didn't tell him about AJ was because Alicia had her thinking he'd found out that AJ wasn't his and I didn't make it no better cause I went along with the shit. Well, I had already let the shit out, might as well finish it.

I began to spot him as he began to force the weight bar up inches from the floor at a time with his leg.

"So how you figure they lied to you?"

He exhaled a deep breath, returned the bar to a resting position and said, "Man... well, I already told you, Alicia told me Terri was like some groupie and shit that use to try to get at me after you got done with her. I guess I kinda saw through that though. I could tell she couldn't stand Terri. The shit showed all over her face."

"Well I guess so. Most women wouldn't be able to stand the woman who went into labor at her weddin' to a nigga she'd been tryin' to get fo' a minute. Then, you left her ass at the alter to go to the hospital with Terri to see yo' shawty bein' born."

His eyes almost popped from his head.

"Yeah nigga, dat's what happened. Let me break it down fo' you. You met Alicia first but didn't get no play off the flip. We met up with her and her sister Punkin at the club to kick it and when you saw her givin' me her number to give to you, cause you was on the dance floor with Terri, you thought we was hollin', so you started kickin' it with Terri. Then you found out that everythang was on the up and up with Alicia and so you kicked it with both of 'em.

Terri had yo' ass mushier than a bowl of whip cream. She had yo' mind gon', sex-wise. Since Alicia wasn't givin' up no ass, tryin' to play the catholic school girl and shit, you kept on kickin' it with Terri."

I patted him on the shoulder.

"I know it's a lot nigga, just try to keep up. Terri came up pregnant and I feel kinda guilty fo' this one cause I tried to get you to talk her into havin' an abortion. I mean, you wasn't ready, true but you wanted to be different than our sorry ass daddy's and be there fo' yo' shawty. You was stressin' nigga, hard and you told her you'd think about it while we were out in the field on one our training exercises. While out there, you wrote both of them a letter cause if I'm not mistakin' you and Alicia had got into it over her titty or somethin' befo' you left."

"What? What kinda shit is that?" he asked almost chuckling.

"Man, she had cancer or somethin' when she was younger and one of her titties is deformed and she wouldn't let you see it or touch it and ya'll had some words cause you had just finally fucked her for the first time on the cab ride home to her house. But when you was trying to go for round two, you wanted to get touchy-feely on the titties and she snapped out on you. Now, while we was out in the field, you wrote 'em both a letter and told Terri you wanted to be there fo' her and the baby and then you wrote Alicia and told her that you had gotten yo' self in a fucked up situation and you really wanted to be with her but you needed to straighten some shit out first. Well, classically, you put the letters in the wrong envelopes and so Alicia got Terri's and Terri got Alicia's.

As you can probably imagine nigga, you caught hell. I mean, as you can see, you and Alicia eventually worked things out but Terri skipped town and had us running round looking fo' her like we was some muthafuckin' private eyes and when she finally showed up, it was yo' weddin' day. But I gotta give it to her, she never sweated you or nothin' like that after yo' shorty was born. In fact, she moved in with yo' moms and ya'll kept kickin' it on the side. All the way up until the accident. You never could let her go… you know, in here."

I pointed to my heart.

"She'd always been there. You know, at first you thought it was just a physical thang but you found out it was more than that. She loved you enough to step aside and let you marry Alicia and just be the chick on the side cause she couldn't stand not being with you at all. You know what Betty said nigga, 'havin' a piece a man is better than havin' no man at all, so I'm a just take what I got and work with it, you feel me?"

I sighed. He signaled for me to help him to sit up so he could rest.

"I feel kind of fucked up about it man cause you was havin' second thoughts about the weddin' in the first damn place but I talked you into goin' on and doin' yo thang cause I cut fo' Alicia at the time and she was on yo' head bout spendin' so much time and money on the baby, so I suggested you gon' and get married so you could get BAQ and base housing. Plus, I mean, you did love her and you wanted to marry her. But in a way, I think it was more so obligation than anything. Nobody was thinkin' bout how all the shit would play out in the long run."

He shook his head.

"Damn, sounds like hella drama."

"Shit nigga, Mary J couldn't fuck wit' ya'll!"

I laughed.

"Naw but seriously though man, both of love 'em you. You just got caught up. I didn't peep how much Terri really loved you until all this went down and now, I got mad respect fo' her."

He lay back down to continue lifting. He was doing good for his first time out. He seem to be only struggling slightly. That was a good sign.

"But that's what so confusing to me "C". If she loved me all like that, then why bullshit me? About us, about the baby... man, she told me I was his fuckin' god-uncle or some shit like that."

I shook my head and laughed.

"Damn," I whispered to myself.

"Aey man, I can't answer that one fo' you playa. But I'm sure it's fo' a good reason. Maybe with everything goin' on she just felt it was best. Switch legs."

"I guess you right," he said as he switched his legs underneath the bar. "I won't say nothin' to her about it then. She'll let me know when she feels its right."

"Yeah, she will. Count on it."

I slapped him five.

"Thanks man, that made shit make a whole lot of sense to me."

"You got it playa."

Chapter Seventeen... Cory

When we finished up Arman's workout, we headed back to the room to find Alicia sitting there, waiting for us. My stomach instantly dropped down into my nuts. She was sitting in the chair, crying her eyes out.

When she noticed us enter the room, she quickly wiped her face and put on a half hearted smile.

"There you are. I've been waiting for you."

Arman' looked to me then back to Alicia.

"You were also crying, what's up?" he asked as I helped him out of his wheelchair. I wanted to know what all the theatrics and hoopla was about myself. I assumed it had something to do with Terri. I turned Arman's body away from her to help him sit down on the bed and Alicia shot me a look that pierced daggers through my body. That's when I knew it had something to do with the baby.

Then just as quickly, she began crying again.

"I don't understand... my baby... our baby's not getting any better."

"Why not? I thought they were gon' transfuse her?"

She looked over to me.

134

"They tried. Same blood type and everything but somehow, she her body still rejected it."

She began to break down uncontrollably.

"How could she reject it? I don't understand that. I mean, that don't sound right."

Arman' stroked her hair and whispered to her.

"She'll be okay. They probably just made a technical error."

He lifted her face to him.

"I'd like to see her if that's aight? What do you think?"

She smiled at that idea.

"I think that's a great idea, man," I cut in.

Alicia shot eyes made of stone at me. I ignored her and continued.

"Why don't you take him up to see the baby, it'll be good for both of 'em."

At that moment, she wanted nothing more than to spit on my grave. She thought I was being hateful but I really wasn't. Not at that moment anyway. I needed her to occupy him for a while cause had something to take care of.

Whats Done In The Dark

"Okay, let's do it."

I helped him sit back in his wheelchair and pushed him out to the nurse's station.

"Aight playa, I got to handle somethin' right quick. I'll be back tomorrow after work. I might be a little late but I'll be here."

"What, you ain't goin' to see my shawty?"

"Umm… naw dawg, that's a whole intimate family thang right there. Ya'll should be alone. But I'll catch up with you tomorrow."

"Aight then," he said, slapping my hand. "Thanks again man, for everything and you know what I mean."

"No doubt dawg, I'm out."

As I watched the nurse pushed him down the hallway towards the elevator, Alicia looked back at me as if she desperately trying to figure it out. She wouldn't have the chance though. When they were out of sight, I dipped up the stairs to the fourth floor lab, entered the brown oak doors and walked over to the counter to speak with the lab technician on duty.

"Yeah, uh… I'm here to give blood fo' baby Jones."

"You the father?" the chubby white male nurse asked.

For the first time since all this started, I accepted my responsibility.

"Yeah man, I'm the father."

He called the NICU to inform them that I was there once again to have my blood drawn. I felt good cause I knew I was doing the right thing. Not for Alicia's trick ass but for Arman'. He didn't need any more stress on him. Dealing with Alicia's bullshit in his current state of mind could damage him beyond compare.

The clerk came back to the counter with a dark and sullen look on his face.

"You ready, man?" I asked him.

I just wanted to get the shit over with before I changed my mind. I was starting to think about the possibility of future responsibilities and I was getting antsy.

"Well, Mr.… Starks, there's no need for us to draw your blood again, Sir."

I was lost. If the baby rejected Earl's blood, naturally I would think they needed more.

"Why is that?"

"Maybe you should go on up to the NICU and let the doctor explain it to you."

"Why can't you explain it to me?"

He sighed.

"It's not my…"

"Man, just come out with the shit."

"I'm… I'm sorry to tell you this but Baby Girl Jones… Baby Girl Jones just died a couple minutes ago. I'm really, really sorry."

I stood there frozen, trying to take in what he'd just said. The baby had died.

My baby?

I mean, abortion was different cause the kid wasn't there but this actually was fucked up. All because I was trying to teach Alicia's ass a lesson for fucking with me.

My baby paid with her life, shit!

I know Arman' was tripping and Alicia, God only knows what she was letting come out of her mouth at that moment. She was totally unstable. I felt like shit in every sense of the word. Especially after the afternoon conversation we'd had during his therapy.

Damn, I'd caused him more pain.

What the fuck is wrong with me?

I had to get outside. I had to smoke. I needed it to give me some clarity on what the hell was going on. But most of all, I needed it to once again; numb the pain I felt inside. The pain... I didn't want to feel the pain...

Chapter Eighteen... Arman'

"... who would've known, that you'd have to go, so suddenly so fast? And now that your gone, everyday I'll go on but life just not the same..."

I sat there, holding a beautiful curly haired princess in a lovely pink, Winnie the Pooh blanket. Alicia had dressed our baby girl in a pretty pink nightie. She was no longer breathing. No signs of life flowing through her body. I felt the loss even though I wasn't attached to her like her mother was. She was so beautiful and memory or not, how could I not love her?

Alicia was terribly upset and she kept mumbling to herself, "I don't understand, I don't understand."

I don't know what that meant but I don't think it was for me to understand. The nurse removed the baby from my arms and Alicia hit the floor. I couldn't get to her, my physical circumstances prohibited me. I called out for her and slowly she came to me. I watched as she crawled across the floor like a wounded animal.

I didn't know what to say to her. I felt only a small fraction of the pain she'd felt at that moment. She looked up to me, eyes engrossed with tears.

"I'm so sorry Arman', this is all my fault. I..."

I placed my finger to her lips.

"Shh, listen to me, this is not your fault. Don't you ever say that again. This is something that was out of yo' control."

She continued to sob, tuning out my every word. I understood that the ordeal with me doubled the loss she was feeling. From what Cory had told me, I'd taken her through hell by cheating on her with Terri and having a baby with her outside our relationship, now this. I know all this was killing her inside. Now she'd lost the one thing she felt connected her to me.

I stroked her face, as I thought back to earlier that day. I felt so bad for what I'd done with Terri but only because of the pain I saw Alicia experiencing at the time. I felt something very strong for Terri and from all I'd heard, I had reason too.

I'd have to put all those feelings on the back burner for now though because my wife needed me to be there for her.

"Arman'... I'm so very sorry. I wanted so badly for us to share what you and Ter..."

She stopped mid-sentence and it seemed as if her whole demeanor changed. She wiped her tears and quickly, too quickly pulled herself together. She stood up and looked down at the empty incubator that once held her bundle of joy.

141

"You don't need to be around all this, you have been through enough and you have enough on yo' plate right now," she told me.

She turned to me.

"Come on, I'll take you back."

I put my hands around her waist and guided her down upon my lap. She rested her head on my shoulders.

"I need to be wherever you are. We did make this baby together, right?"

She stared off at the wall and shook her head. She couldn't look at me so I forced her face towards mine.

"Aight then, we'll go though this together. You wanna call yo' family so they can come and be with you?"

She nodded her head in agreement.

"I'll call mine and you do the same, aight?"

She rose to her feet.

"Aey, Alicia…"

She turned to me.

"When I get better, we can always try again."

"Again?" she whispered.

She looked so crushed and defeated.

"Yeah, again. I didn't get a chance to tell you but earlier that I got some of the feeling back in my legs. So yeah, I mean, it may take a lil time but when I'm at one hundred, we can get pregnant again. Well, I mean you."

She smiled.

"I mean, we have plenty of time, it's no hurry. It's yo' decision."

Her smile broadened.

"Arman', you're one of the sweetest men I've ever known and I love you so much for simply the suggestion."

Our families arrived within the hour. Everyone was there except for Cory and Terri. He didn't show up to the grave side service we held that following Saturday either but Terri did. She refused to make eye contact with me. Probably was for the best because if I locked eyes with her once, I'd never turn away.

As they lowered the tiny, white casket into the ground, the sun shined down on the small golden angels that encamped around it. I sat beside Alicia in my wheelchair and held her tightly in my arms, allowing her to cry out all the pain she was feeling inside.

My moms stood at the head of the casket and sang a beautiful rendition of "Eye on the Sparrow."

My eyes watered. I wanted so badly to remember my life before the crash. I wanted to share her pain but I couldn't. My mind had me limited. Limited to it's own incompetence.

As the service ended and all the people came to us to say goodbye and extend their well wishes, Terri approached us along side of Pooh. As Pooh hugged Alicia and they cried together, Terri finally looked at me. I could feel her heart reaching out to me. Her desire to hold me and show me how much she cared for me.

"I'm… I'm very sorry for yo' loss," she said through tears streaming down her face.

Before I could respond, Alicia broke loose from Pooh and lit into Terri with a vengeance.

"You had no right coming here to my baby's funeral! I can't believe I couldn't even bury my own baby without you being around. Do you want him that bad? That bad, that you gotta stalk him at our baby's funeral? Huh Terri? You never cease to fuckin' amaze me!

Messin' up my wedding wasn't good enough for you? Keeping him out at all times of the night, you and that, that…"

She caught herself.

144

"You disgust me, you really disgust me."

Then it happened. I don't think anyone was prepared for it, it just happened. Alicia hurled a wad of saliva from her lips that landed on Terri's right eye. Pooh grabbed Terri and Donna, my oldest sister, whom I'd met for the first time that morning, grabbed Alicia.

"No Pooh, I'm cool. I'm cool," Terri said.

She wiped her face with a tissue my momma gave her and looked to me.

"Try not to see the loss of my child as an opportunity for you to try to work yo' way into his pants again. Because as soon as he gets better, he's already promised me another one."

Terri's eyes shot to mine as they welled up with tears. She stepped back and turned to leave, not wanting Alicia to know she'd gotten the best of her by breaking her down. She walked away with the utmost class and dignity and I have to be honest, I was outdone. Mourning or not, I couldn't have taken it but that just showed me why I was so crazy about her. She wasn't into the drama.

Pooh looked to Alicia.

"Look Alicia, I know you're hurting and all that but what you just did was both uncalled for and wrong. She came here with me, to be with me while *I* said goodbye to my niece. Arman' can't even remember he fucked the damn girl. That shit was childish and just plain foul. I expected better from you."

As she walked away, I overheard her asking Terri if she wanted her to get AJ from the pastor's wife.

AJ, my son? My son's here?

I watched Pooh's every move until she held in her arms, the most handsome little baby boy. He had long curly hair, Carmel complexion and looked a lot like his mother. He was asleep and he looked so adorable.

I wanted to go over to him and grab him but Terri hadn't felt comfortable enough to tell me the truth about him yet. Besides, Alicia had a death grip on me since she'd seen Terri there and it wouldn't have been right for me to leave her in her time of need.

I followed them with my eyes until they got into the limo and drove away. I turned to Alicia. Now that everyone was out of ear shot range, I wanted to know what the hell that was all about and see if she was gonna be woman enough to tell me.

"Why did you act like that? That wasn't cool, at all. I mean, even if she tried to get with me, ruin our marriage or whatever, I can't remember it. I can't remember her. I'm getting' to know her all over again and I think she's good people. I like her. But that's

146

neither here nor there. So why are you makin' a public spectacle of yo'self when you suppose to be in mournin'. I don't get it… that was so uncalled for and unfair."

"Unfair? What's unfair is that my baby is in the ground, never to come back. I don't have what she has."

It only took me a moment to realize she was talking about AJ but she didn't know that I already knew that he was my son.

"What does she have?"

I wanted to here her say it. Own up to what they lied to me about. She placed her hands up.

"You know what, it doesn't even matter. I just need to go on home and rest. I'm sorry Arman', really I am. I'm just so stressed out and depressed these days with all that has happened and I guess I needed to vent and I took it out on her."

I gripped her hand.

"I understand all that but you can't go around wanting innocent people to hurt because you hurt. You can't do that, aight?"

She shook her head in agreement.

"Aey, do you know why Cory didn't show up?"

Once again, she went into flip mode on me.

"No and I don't give a damn!"

Now what the fuck was that about?

She must have noticed the look on my face and quickly, she calmed down.

"Look honey, I'm just tired and I'm snappy. I'm a call you up at the hospital as soon as I think you've made it back. Unless, you want me to ride in the Medic Van with you?"

From behind us, Cory appeared.

"Naw, it's cool, I got 'em."

Their eyes locked for a brief moment and hatred was all I seen.

What is up with them?

Alicia kissed me on the lips.

"I'll call you soon, okay?'

"You aight? If not, you can roll up to the hospital and chill with me, cool? I mean it, don't hesitate."

"Okay."

148

I kissed her again and watched her walk away and get into the awaiting limo.

When she disappeared, Cory walked over to the casket and watched as the workers began to throw dirt down on top of the casket. He stared down and I could tell he was a little shook up.

"So where you been man? How come you just now comin' through?"

He turned around and walked over to me.

"I don't deal well with loss. Stems back from my pops walkin' out on us, I guess. Besides, this here was a private thang, fo' you, yo' family; Alicia and her fam."

"What's up with ya'll, man?" I asked as he pushed me over towards his white Isuzu jeep.

"Why ya'll act like ya'll can't stand the sight of each other?'

"It's a long story, playa."

"It's a long ride," I answered.

Chapter Nineteen... Terri

"... we use to talk and laugh all night girl, what happened to those days, did they all just fade away..."

I'd had it! I couldn't take no more. That bitch spit on me, spit on me! She didn't miss an opportunity to tear me down in front of Arman'. And he just sat there and said nothing. Memory or not, I didn't have to take shit from her.

Who the hell did she think she was?

I was so sick and tired of that bitch. I laid back in the limo as we rode along the highway.

"You know she's just going through some things Terri, don't let her get to you," Pooh said. "You know where stand with him right? You just gotta hold on to that."

I tried to calm down but I was livid.

"Certain peoples grieve in certain ways baby," Momma J stated. "Only God knows what's inside a person's heart. Manni' loves you very much chil', you know dat. But he's got to 'onor his responsibilities to his wife also. Don't worry chil', thangs will work themselves out. God is an on time God. You can't rush 'em but he'll be there."

She patted me on the knee and started humming. She always uplifted me.

"Please, hurry God," I mumbled to myself.

I held AJ close to me and silently prayed for all of this to end. Why couldn't things just go back to normal? I missed Arman', AJ and I spending time as a family. I closed my eyes as **BloodStone** laid out my feelings over the airways.

"*... you and me girl, go a long way back. And I'm so proud, I'm so proud. You and me girl, go along way back. I remember, when loving you wasn't easy, it wasn't easy baby,*"

I placed AJ on the bed and the phone rang.

"Hello?"

"Hello, Terri, it's me. It's Arman'."

My heart skipped a beat and totally left my mind on its own to be upset with him.

"How are you feeling," I asked him.

"Not to well. It's mentally more so than physically. I had another flashback episode."

"Really? Anything new?"

"Yeah, I could see myself leaving the hospital."

"Were you upset, can you remember?"

He sighed.

"Naw."

I lay back on the bed beside AJ and picked up the framed picture of him and Arman'. I felt so bad for giving him that cough syrup so he'd sleep during the funeral and not start hollering for his father. If he'd laid eyes on him, it would have been over. I ran my fingers across his face, realizing then that I couldn't expect Arman' to fight for me. He couldn't even remember the love we had for one another. He only suspected it.

"Terri, are you there?"

I placed the picture back on the nightstand.

"Yeah, I'm here."

"Look, I'm so sorry for all that drama out at the cemetery. I can't get with Alicia's behavior. I mean, Cory explained some of it to me but I'm still kinda thrown for a loop."

"It okay, I've kinda gotten use to it," I lied.

I wanted to tell him how much I wanted to rip the bitch's lips off her face but I wanted him, as always to see me as the bigger woman, even if she was his wife.

"You know how it is when two women love the same man, there's bound to be drama," I chuckled.

"Ummm, I was wanderin'; Cory says he can't make it to help me with therapy tomorrow. You think you can come by and lend me a hand?"

I didn't hesitate to say yes. After all, it wasn't Alicia he called, it was me.

"Sure, what time?"

"Around two?"

"Two's fine, I'll be there."

"I apologize again… and thanks."

"Arman', please stop thanking me. I'll always be here when you need me. You just get some rest and be ready for tomorrow."

The phone went dead and so did my anger. I loved him too much to be upset with him. I really felt bad for them losing their child because I couldn't imagine losing AJ. He and his father was my world, all I had come to live and breathe for.

My heart ached at the thought of him promising to try to have a baby again with Alicia. I understood that she was his wife and he wanted to do right by her as well but it just slapped me in the face with the reality that even without his memory, I'd never have him the way I wanted… all to myself.

Chapter Twenty...Arman'

"...for you I'd give a lifetime of fedelity, now and for eternity. Cause nothin' is impossible for you, I'll take heart and hand and everything and add to it a weddin' ring..."

Cory had told me the story of how Alicia blamed him for hooking me up with Terri. He had told me how much Terri had taken so much abuse and bullshit from Alicia since our baby had been born and how much Terri had truly loved me. They both did, he explained. He informed me that I never could choose between the two and I had simply refused to let either one of them leave my life. I had to have them both in my world.

I understood that because I was experiencing similar feelings now. I didn't feel that way for the same reasons I'm sure but here of late, I seemed to be torn between the two of them again.

By right, I knew I needed to stand by my wife and be everything she needed me to be but something kept constantly pulling me towards Terri.

She was punctual as usual for therapy. There was tension in the air, I'm sure from what had happened at the cemetary yesterday with Alicia. She seemed distant as she raised my left leg in the air towards my chest for stretching. Her mind was occupied and it showed. I lay there thinking, wondering rather, what my life was like when I was with her.

I thought back to the day she bathe me. If nothing else I knew we had no issues in the bedroom.

"Wanna try the walking bars first today," she asked me, extending her hands to me.

"Depends? You ready to tell me what's on yo' mind?"

"Nothing, I…"

I pulled her down beside me on the royal blue floor mat.

"You're lyin'. Somethin' on yo' mind. Now, if you don't want to tell me, just say you don't want to tell me but don't say nothin's wrong when it's clearly written all over yo' face that somethin' botherin' you."

She laid her head on my chest and I placed my arm around her.

"There's just so much you don't understand. So much I can't talk to you about."

"Why you feel you can't talk to me? Cause I can't remember certain things right now? If you feel I can't understand, make me understand. I didn't lose my common sense. Look Terri, over time with or without amnesia, memories fade okay. But I can't let that get to me. I can't let that stop me making new ones.

Everything I know about you, I've found out from everyone else, especially all the inimate shit. You say you love me but you won't let me in. You're shuttin' me out for reasons, you're right, I don't understand. You lied to me about us being friends, then you allowed me to make love to you, with little if any objections, then you shut me out again. What is it? Talk to me baby, help me feel you."

I felt her tears run across my neck. I squeezed her tightly.

"I know I'm not making any of this any easier for you. It's just that I want to concentrate on getting you better. I don't want to add any stress on you. My problems can wait."

"Says who?"

She pulled away from me and stood to her feet in front of me. Her frame looking dazzling in the black spandex jumper she was wearing. She held her hands out to me again.

"Says me. Besides, we're here to get you together, not me."

I grabbed her hand and she pulled me up into the sitting position. She rolled my wheelchair over and locked it behind me. I pulled myself up into the chair, she pushed me over to the walking bars and locked my chair.

"So, what makes you think I can just concentrate on me when you goin' through somethin'? I mean, if we so close, how could you possibly expect me to pretend that yo' issues ain't important to me?"

With her assistance, I pulled myself up on the bars. I stumbled a little but I quickly caught my balance.

"I didn't say it wasn't important to you honey, I just..."

She was inches away from my face and her sentence was left hanging in the air.

"You just what? Afraid?"

I tried to place my wheight down on my legs but the pain was pretty intense. My face showed the discomfort.

"If it hurts that bad, maybe we should try something else."

"Grab my waist."

"Huh?" she asked.

"Wrap yo' arms around my waist and that'll take some of the pressure off."

Her body pressed close to mine and brought her lips even closer. She was noticeably nervous.

"Now what?" she asked.

"Kiss me."

"Kiss you?"

"Yeah, for every step I take, I want a kiss."

She smiled.

"It'll give me an incentive. Ready?"

I gripped the rails tightly. She nodded her head. I concentrated on lifting my leg while staring at her beautiful, full lips. I gradually lifted my right foot up and slowly dragged it a couple of inches.

"You did it Arman', you took a step baby!"

I waited patiently for my reward. She squeezed my waist and playfully planted a kiss on my lips. I lifted the left leg, repeated the motion and waited for our lips to meet again.

Step... kiss, step... kiss, step... kiss. By the tenth step, our tongues were locked in a wrestling hold. Dancing romantically as if it was the first time we'd tasted each other. She tasted like a cool slice of watermelon on a hot summers day. Her hands moved up my back and the weight slightly shifted. She dug her nails in my back and my jimmy stood out rock solid. She pulled back, looked down and smiled.

"Ummm, glad to see you again."

She placed her hand inside my pants.

"Umm, even happier to feel you again," I said, trying to hold onto the bars.

She kneeled down on her knees and pulled my jimmy from my blue Nike sweats and blue silk boxers. She placed her tongue at the tip and began to swirl it around the head of my jimmy. She created a whirlwind as she inhaled bringing a tingling sensation to my body. Her hummer felt so damn good. She went down to the bottom and let her tongue trace the vein up the center. Then with a strong sucking force, she engulped me all the way back to her throat,

She rolled her tongue underneath the center as her throat muscles massaged its head. I moaned out in ectasy. My palms were so sweaty against the wood and I didn't know how much longer I could hold on.

"Damn that feels good baby, don't stop."

She found her rythmn and took me where I wanted to go. My legs buckled underneath me she had me going so good. She jumped to her feet.

"Are you okay?"

I leaned in to kiss her. The flavor of my jimmy on her lips excited me. She pulled back.

"Arman', I'm serious, if this is hurting you…"

"Oh, it wasn't the pain that made my knees buckle."

She hit me on the arm. I pointed to the mat on the floor with a nodd of my head. She smiled.

"Wait here a sec."

She went over, picked up the mat and slid it over directly underneath me.

"You think anyone will come check on us?"

"You think I care," I told her.

"Enough said."

I let my weight drop down onto the mat. I slid back and let my back rest up against the wall for support.

Terri unfastened the buttons on her jumper and seductively slid it down her body. She had her back to me and bent down to remove the jumper from her ankles, exposing the pretty universe between her legs. My mouth instantly watered.

I instructed her to come over to me, place her hands on the bars and spread her legs apart. I ran my hands up her legs and thighs until I reached her overflowing ocean. I placed my first two fingers inside. It was warm and inviting. She moaned out my name.

"Oh Arman', that feels so good."

I brung her body to my face and gripped her clit with my mouth. I devoured it with the tip of my tongue. She squirmed to get loose but I had her legs on lock.

The combination of my fingers and my tongue brought her to a climax.

"Oh, oh, baby... I'm... I'm comin'... oh daddy... oh baby..."

Her legs follwed suit as they caved in and her body fell on top of mine. Our lips met immediately and went to work. She straddled her legs across my lap and I placed my jimmy inside.

Simply put, it was heaven. I gripped her waist and began the rythmn we needed to take us to paradise. She followed brilliantly. The way she moved her body from front to back, side to side, wouldn't allow me to grab a hold of what I felt inside. She was breathtaking. She grabbed my tongue between her lips and began to suck it as she locked her legs behind my back and rode me Derby style.

"Terri, why won't you let me inside you?"

She panted.

"You are…"

"No," I paused.

"I'm not. I'm not talkin' bout physically. I'm talkin' bout inside yo' heart, yo' head… yo' world. Why won't you let me in? What's holdin' you back? On the real, what is it you so scared of?"

She stopped movement and dropped her head. I placed my finger underneath her chin and forced her to face me.

"Terri, baby there is nothin', not now… not tommorrow, not even when my memory comes back that I could find out about you and not still want you in my life."

She raised her eyes to mine.

"What about your wife? Memories or not, you're still attached. And don't get me wrong, I'd never jepardize that in any way but eventually…"

I placed my finger to her mouth.

"I don't know what goin' on between us, me and her. All I know is that at some point in time, I must've loved her very much or she wouldn't be my wife. And I know she's goin' through it right now, with the baby and me. This isn't an issue to press with her at this time. I'm sorry if that hurt your feelings. Believe me,

I'm not tryin' too. But I also know that somethin's gotta give, that I do know."

I touched her face slowly and gently.

"Because I can't give this up. I can't give you up. From what I've been told, I never could. Granted, it is pretty fucked up that I put you in this situation both now and back then. For that, I am truly sorry."

"You didn't put me in anything. I'm a big girl and I could've walked away if I wanted too. I actually tried to, on more than one occasion but I always came back. My love for you wouldn't allow me to stay away, it still won't. I guess I've loved you for so long, the shit just won't go away."

"I'm glad."

I kissed her hard on the mouth and she instantly began the rythmn again. She was putting her all into every stroke. I released her lips. Her body was taking my breath away. The more she thrust, the closer I came to explosion.

"Terri... baby, I... I... I can't hold it... Boo... its cummin' baby, its..."

"Cum for me baby... cum in yo' pussy. It's yours, it'll always be yours," she panted.

My body trembled, my mouth dried, sweat pouring from my forehead. I let it go and the moment I did, my mind flashed back to a scene when we had apparently made love.

We were lying on the floor in front of the TV. Terri was wearing a gold silk robe. We were in the exact same position with my back up against the couch.

"Terri?"

"Yeah baby," she answered, with her head lying on my shoulder.

We were both still trying to catch our breath.

"You own a gold robe of some sort?"

She sprang up.

"A gold robe, um hum, why?"

It hit her.

"You remember it?"

"Yeah, I saw us making love in this same position, on white or off white carpet. You had on a gold robe."

She hugged me tightly.

"You remembering baby! That's my house with the crème colored carpet. It's coming back Arman'. That's the night Alicia went into labor. That's wonderful baby you can re…"

She got silent and gripped her chest as if she'd seen a ghost.

"Umm… maybe, we should get back to the room. You know Momma J is due here any minute. It's after three."

She tried to get up but I grabbed her arms.

"See, there you go again. What was that thought all about before you just flipped the script like that. What is it about my memory that scares you?"

She shook her head.

"No… nothing."

"Don't lie to me Terri. I'm beggin' you, please don't lie to me."

"It's nothing Boo, really," she paused. "I guess I'm just afraid that… well, when your memory comes back. You'll remember how much you loved Alicia and I'll lose you again."

"Aey," I said holding her tightly. "That's not gonna happen, I promise."

I kissed her on the cheek.

"Ok?"

She shook her head.

I released her to get dressed and I pulled myself back up in my wheelchair. I watched her as she moved about to straighten back up the room. I longed to make all this right, especially between us. But she had to be honest with me, all the way, before I knew the right steps to take. She had to let me inside before I could do anything.

The family was waiting for us when we reached the room, which gave Terri the perfect excuse to dip. Something was up with her. She was hiding something from me that she felt could destroy her in my eyes.

But what?

The entire time the family was visiting, my mind stayed on Terri and this secret of hers.

What could it be? Why can't she just trust me enough to be honest with me?

I didn't know how but the next opportunity was mine to find out what the hell was going on...

Chapter Twenty One... Terri

"... love, there's so many things I've got to tell you but I'm afraid I don't know how cause there's a possibilty that you'll look at me differently, love..."

His memory was slowly beginning to return to him.

What did life hold in store for me once it did?

He would be sure to leave me once his mind began feeding him those doubts again. How in God's name could Arman' think that AJ wasn't his son? We'd stopped using condoms because he knew he was the only one I was sleeping with.

My mind wondered a million places as I walked down the corridor. I passed the chapel once, twice... three times before I finally went inside. I kneeled down at the altar and hesistantly began to pray.

"God, if you can hear me, I need you to please show me what to do here. How do I fix this? Once Arman's memory returns God, I've lost him for good. I don't know what to do. Please, tell me what to do."

The tears began to flow down my face.

"He's the only man I've ever loved."

I tried to gain my composure but I couldn't. I felt my world falling apart. The hurt was overwhelming. New hurt... past hurt. After all those years, still fresh.

How could God allow it to happen to me?

I felt so out of place for praying to him, yet, I did my best. I had to try to focus on the future and not the past. But the pain was still so very real and it made the fear of losing Arman' seem impossible to bear.

I was just a ten year old, bright eyed little girl. So full of hopes and dreams. Shattered by a drunken step-father. Those nights never left me.

It began with a stolen glance while mom wasn't looking, an univiting glance. As he pounded away at my ten year old fragile body, oblivious to the pain he was causing me, he spoke these words to me.

"You'll never be able to keep a man if you can't fuck'em right. Yo'momma... she can't fuck worth shit. I been waitin' for this day. I'ma teach you how to keep a man happy. I want you to be a big girl and dry those tears. It won't hurt, I promise."

I felt the reason my mother agreed for me to marry so young is because she knew the things that were happening to me and instead of dealing with it, she just wanted to get rid of me.

My ex-husband taught me everything else I needed to know about sex. My drunken step-father's words always burned inside my head.

You'll never keep a man if you can't fuck 'em right.

So I used what I knew best to get Arman' and to keep him. There were no limits to our sexual excapades in the bedroom. I always pulled out all the stops. It wasn't until he found me in Dallas, after he'd finally married Alicia, that Arman' told me that the reason he loved me wasn't physical, at least not any more.

"Terri, you never had to pretend with me. You were fine, just being yourself. The night we met, I thought I was just physically attracted to you. You were so beautiful to me. Yes, you made love to me like no other woman I've ever been with, but when you left this time, I realized that it was nothing sexual I missed about you.

And I'm thankful that we didn't give in to our attraction for each other since the baby's been born because it's allowed me to see that there's so much more between us. I missed the way your hum in the shower, the love you show my moms and my family. I miss watching you bathe AJ and feed him. I missed talking to you and laughing with you.

You became one of my best friends. Terri, I know there's so much more to you than just sex. You're very intelligent and bright.

It takes a special breed of women to date Uncle Sam. You're wonderful baby, both inside and out."

He loved me, pure and simple.

But for how long? Until he gets his memory back, then what? I'll lose him again, for sure.

I couldn't allow that to happen. I had to find a way to make things right.

"I'm counting on you God. I need your help. Please, show me how to make this work."

I rose up from the altar and headed out the chapel, down to my car. As I turned on the ignition, I sat back and absorbed the sounds of **Ann Nesby**.

"... she can't love you like I do. You thought that she could do the things I do. She can't hold you like I do... she can't, she can't..."

I turned off the ignotion and headed back inside the hospital doors. This was my last chance at love and I refused to let it go without a fight. I had come too far, suffered too much. As I made my way to the lab, I knew in my heart, God was showing me how to get what it was I so desperately wanted... my family back.

Chapter Twenty Two...Cory

"... I had to meet you here today, there is just so many things to say. Please don't stop me 'til I am through, this is somethin' I hate to do..."

I sat there in my barracks room on the couch, getting high again. My thoughts fading in the background, giving way to the mellow feeling my new found love had brought me. This was all getting to be too much to handle. Arman', the baby, Alicia, Pooh... I saw no end to the drama and the pain it caused.

2Pac played over the speakers as I inhaled another hit off the Cain laced joint.

"... now we was once two nigga's of the same kind. Quick to holla at a hoochie with the same line. I could see us after school we'd bomb, on the first muthafucka with the wrong shit on..."

The situation with my baby fucked me up more than I was willing to both accept and admit. But it was all over now, never to be brought up again.

Knock, knock.

Damn, who the fuck is this?

I knew it couldn't have been Pooh because she was still at the hospital with Arman'. She had just hung up the phone a few minutes ago. Other women wasn't stupid enough to just show up unannounced at my door, none but one.

171

I put out my spliff and took a swallow of Hennessey from the shot glass on the table in front of me. I walked over to the door, opened it and instantly got sick to my stomach.

"We need to talk," Alicia said as she stormed inside, She threw her purse on the couch and stood there, hands on her hips.

"And I want some fucking answers!"

I closed the door behind her and sat back down on the couch. I knew this would come eventually. I looked up to her.

"First of all, don't be comin' up in my room like you bout it and shit demandin' a muthafuckin' thang from me! Second, what the fuck do you want?"

"I wanna know why my daughter rejected your blood?"

I leaned forward and took another swig of Hennessey.

"Shit, I don't know, you tell me. I did my part. I mean, me and my boy was the only ones you was fuckin', right?"

She reached over and slapped the drink out of my hand causing it to splatter across the table and the floor.

"Fuck you Cory! What the hell is that supposed to mean?"

I rose up from the couch, just in case I was about to have to man handle the bitch.

"Look Alicia, you pissin' me off. I did what you asked aight, I got the baby some blood. What the hell else do you want from me?"

"The truth Cory, I want the truth. I want you to tell me why she wouldn't take your blood. What happened?"

My blood began to boil.

"How the fuck should I know? I ain't no fuckin' doctor. This is the shit *you* asked for. I told yo' ass from jump not to try to trap that nigga but you was so busy tryin' to compete with a muthafuckin' broad that nigga was gon' be with reguardless. I told you long time ago, let that shit ride. A muthafuckin' dog roams from home all the time but when it can find its own way back, you got that muthafucka trained. Point is, who gave a fuck what that nigga was doin' in the streets, he bought his ass and his money home to you everynight. But you, like most women wasn't happy with that. Now look…"

I was pacing back and forth in front of her, hands going everywhere, emphasazing every word.

"You had a choice to accept the shit or roll on. You chose to accept it but then you try this stupid shit. Now the shit backfires and you wanna blame me? What the fuck did you expect Alicia? You bought this shit on yo' self. Now, you want me to make all this shit go away, how? How the fuck you expect me to do that?"

She was balling out of control and I knew she wanted me to comfort her but I couldn't. It meant accepting some of the blame and I just couldn't bring myself to do that. This shit had gotten out of hand and it all could've been avoided had she listened to me in the first damn place. She's the one who put us in the cross. I felt little, if any sympathy for her at all.

Deep inside I knew I was just as much at fault as she was but all this could've been shut down from day one with a little over three hundred dollars. Now everybody was in pain. Her, Arman' Terri, AJ, the family and me. It all had a trickle down effect I hadn't realized before.

"Something went wrong Cory and you know what that something is. I know you, you've got too."

"Look Alicia, it's to damn late to worry about all that shit now. He told you ya'll could try again when his health permits. He's gettin' stronger everyday, so why not just chill and do shit the right way this time around. This is over, it's done. It can't be fixed. And if I was you, on the serious tip, I'd try to get pregnant before his memory comes back cause after that, you can hang it up. You assed out."

She walked over to the couch, grabbed her purse and headed towards the door. She stopped, turned around, threw her purse back onto the couch and walked over to me. She slid her hands up my chest, raised her eyes to mine and through tears, she asked me to be with her.

"Can't we just forget about all them Cory? Can't you make another baby with me? Wouldn't that be so much easier? I mean you did say you loved me, right?"

Never tell a woman you love her if you don't mean it. Cause if you do, you'll end up dealing with shit like this.

174

"That way, we won't have to worry about his memory or the family. It could be just us."

She was attempting to kiss my neck. My head without the brain was in agreement with her as he bulged out from underneath my black silk boxers and pressed against her waist. She reached down and gripped my jimmy tightly. The feel of her touch was different. It was both cold and unwanted. I grabbed her arms and pulled back.

"Aey, back up off me. I don't wanna do this with you. Not now, not ever. This bullshit right here, will never happen again. I suggest you find some other sucka to get this time cause it won't be me."

Within an instant, she went from the poor mistreated little girl to the bitch from hell.

"Oh, so you sayin' fuck me now, right?"

"Aey, take it how you wanna take it, this is just the way it's gotta be. We've done enough damage and I ain't goin' out like that no mo'. Not wit' yo' trick ass."

Her eyes were dark and as cold as stone. She walked back over to the couch, grabbed her purse again and reached for the door knob.

"I don't know how but I promise you Cory, you will pay for this. You the last motherfucka to fuck over me. That, I can promise you."

She slammed the door behind her and left me to dwell on that statement. I pondered it for a moment then I brushed it off my shoulder.

That hoe ain't built like that and she ain't bout it enough to roll like that. If she was, she wouldn't have let Queen B steal her man in the first fuckin' place. I tried to reassure my self.

I reloaded my drink and re-lit my spliff and as I continued to bump Pac on the stereo, I chased my joints with plenty of Hennessey.

Deep down inside, I tried to fight my gut feeling that this shit wasn't really over. That Alicia, would definitely live to reign again.

Chapter Twenty Three...Terri

"... How could you deny, your own flesh and blood? She said it's your child, staring at me with eyes like yours..."

I went up to the fourth floor lab to find Dr. Campbell. I had to find out about the blood tests he ran on Arman' and AJ. The small, elderly white nurse sat behind the desk, pecking on the computer. I approached her and asked if it would possible to speak with the doctor, explaining to her that he'd delivered my baby a while back and the baby was now having some difficulties.

I stood by anxiously as she paged him and we awaited his call back. My mind was racing with thoughts of earlier that day. Arman', the love we made and how our souls still connected even though his mind couldn't remember. I loved him so much and for all our sakes, especially AJ's, I had to find the error in those test results.

The doctor called back and said he'd be right up. I pulled up a chair in the lobby area and watched a little TV until he made it. When he greeted me, I asked him to please excuse me for showing up unannounced.

"There's a problem that can't wait any longer."

"Well, I hope I can help Ms. Lambert, follow me."

We entered his office and I took a seat, noticing the wall he'd dedicated to all the children he'd delivered since being on staff there. I wondered was AJ's picture up there. I walked over and began to search across the faces of all the beautiful children. All different shades of perfect colors.

"You delivered all these babies in just two years?"

"Yeah and I have more to still pin up. It's definitely the baby booming era."

I smiled as I finally spotted the picture of my handsome prince the day he was born. His pink complexion and beautiful curly hair. Under his picture read, "Baby Boy Jones."

I continued to scan the board as I began to talk to the doctor as to why I came to him seeking his assistance.

"Doctor Campbell, do you recall if someone requested some DNA tests done recently on my son?"

"No ma'am, not off the top of my head."

"But if they had, you would've been the one to handle it, right? I mean, since you delivered my son and you being his acting Pediatrician, right?"

"Not necessarily, it depends if I was on duty at the time of the request. We have three more Doctors that could've handled that. But I could have his chart pulled for you and check."

"Could you please," I said, fumbling impatiently with my fingers. He picked up the phone to order AJ's medical chart as my eyes rested on a tiny, familiar face on his wall. It was the photo of a tiny baby girl in an incubator. She was so small and looked so fragile. The card underneath read, "Babygirl Jones."

"I didn't know you delivered this baby also," I said as he hung up the phone.

"Yeah, one of those rare cases where the baby was born with antibodies to the mother's own blood. I'll never forget that case. We tried and tried to transfuse her with the father's blood but it didn't work, the blood didn't match."

I almost passed out. I must have heard him wrong.

Did he say that the blood didn't match?

I dug a little deeper.

"That's impossible, I know this couple Doctor Campbell. Are you sure we're talking about the same baby?"

"Babygirl Jones, who just recently passed away because her white blood cells started attacking her own vital organs, that's her."

"But how is it possible the blood donor didn't match?"

"Look Ms. Lambert, I can't discuss this with you any further. I've already said some things that I shouldn't have said on the issue. Let's just wait on the chart to come up."

I placed my hands on his desk, covering up the paperwork he was attempting to read.

"You don't understand," I began frantically.

"Look at the last names. Our children share the same father, or so I thought. Please doctor, can you just explain to me why it was possible the results didn't match… please."

I pleaded with him and tried desperately to make him feel my pain. See how important this really was to me. He sighed.

"Well, the concept is, is that there was another donor. A sperm donor that is. All I know is, I was the one who had to tell that soldier that the babygirl he was so crazy about, wasn't his."

I couldn't believe my ears.

Alicia's baby wasn't Arman's? Whose was it then?

"Are you sure? Can you pull that baby's chart also?"

"No ma'am, I can not. But I can assure you, I'm correct."

Just then, the nurse knocked on the door to bring the chart he'd ordered. He began to thumb through for lab work as I stared out the window in disbelief.

What the hell was going on? Why didn't Arman' tell me? That had to be the reason he was speeding in such a rage. He was going to tell Cory about the baby.

"Umm, Ms. Lambert, I don't see any blood tests ordered for you son ma'am. Are you sure we did the tests here?"

I stood there, engulfed in rage.

So, it was her child's results all along that had Arman' in such an uproar and damn near cost him his life. He never had a chance to tell anyone else about the blood tests so she figured she could throw the blame on me. She expected him to die and thought that no one would ever find out.

That sadistic bitch! All this time, taking advantage of his mental state of mind and playing the role. And to think I actually felt sorry for her ass when the baby died.

I'd given up the man I loved again, so she could be with him and for what?

A lie?

It was all a lie. I had to tell Arman', but how?

Would he believe me?

I had to figure out something because we were all fooled. I thanked the doctor for his time and all his help. I headed for the elevator and down to my car. I was steaming. That bitch had played the role perfectly... but guess what?

"Your movie is about to be pulled bitch and I got the plug in my hand..."

Chapter Twenty Four...Terri

"...you're my little secret and that's how we should keep it. We should never let 'em know about you and I, You're my little secret..."

Three months had passed since I'd found out about Arman' and Alicia's baby. I didn't want to break the news to Arman' while he was in the hospital and still trying to focus on getting better. His memory was returning in bits and pieces.

He was finally home now and now it was time to make my move. I pulled up into Momma J's driveway. I parked the car and went inside. Everyone was out back for Arman's welcome home party, chit-chatting around the barbeque grill. I had stopped by the Carter's to pick up AJ on the way over. It would be the first time Arman' would come face to face with his son since the crash.

Your son... this one's all yours.

I stood on the other side of the sliding door in the kitchen and watched the scene. Alicia was snuggled up under Arman's arm on the two-man oak swing. I cringed my teeth and shook my head in disgust. I was so sick of her taking him for granted.

Abusing his love and honor for her own sick and twisted purposes. But it was all about to come to an end.

I walked onto the back porch and pressed a smile as Arman's eyes locked with mine. He immediately removed his arm from around Alicia and her face grimaced at the sight of me. One

182

thing was for certain, this family loved me like one of their own so it would be no getting out of line with me, not today.

"Hey girl, where you been? What took you so long," Pooh asked.

"It's funny you should ask me that Pooh."

I picked up the remote to the stereo system Momma J was using to play her favorite backyard music, the blues. I hit the button to turn off the system and when I did, all eyes fell on me.

"I've been up at the hospital, inquiring about the blood work Arman' had done on AJ, according to Alicia," I lied.

I couldn't let them know I'd been hiding information for three months. Cory's face frowned immediately and Pooh seemed sorta offended.

"You see," I started again, waving inside for Momma J to bring AJ outside to me. Arman' became bright eyed as he watched her place the handsome toddler in my arms.

"This here," I began, pointing to AJ.

"Is Arman's son."

Arman' grabbed his walking braces and slowly stood to his feet. When AJ saw his daddy, he began to squirm and cry for him. Arman' slowly struggled over to us, staring at AJ and I, confused.

"Terri, you didn't have to go through all that. We never doubted you." Pooh answered.

"My son? This is my son?"

Arman' looked to Cory and Cory smiled. Then he looked to me and his smile suddenly faded.

"Terri, maybe it's time you told me what's goin' on. I mean, you told me…"

I turned to him.

"I know what I told you baby but I lied. And I'm sorry but I lied because you were sick and Alicia told us all that it was my fault that you had the accident because you'd found out that AJ wasn't your son and you were speeding to tell Cory and you crashed. But he is your son, every drop of blood that runs through his veins is yours. You knew that because you never ordered any tests done on him, ain't that right, Alicia?"

Everyone turned towards the swing but Alicia was no longer there. I guess she knew her time had come and rather face what was about to go down, the bitch ran like a little coward.

"Now hold on here a minute. Terri, what are you's tryin' to tell us?"

Momma J was as confused as Arman'.

"Hol' up," Arman' interupted before I could answer her.

"All this time you got me thinkin' that I'm trippin about what's been between us but on the real, you was keepin' my own son from me cause of what somebody told you? Hell Terri, this was the time I needed to spend with my son the most. I trusted you and you play me like a fool? What the hell is that about?"

"This is what the fuck it's about!"

All heads turned as Alicia stood in the doorway with a small, silver plated gun in her hand, aimed directly at us all.

"Chil' what the devil is wrong wit' you? You put that thang down this instant!"

"I'm sorry Momma J, I can't do that. It's all out now. Well, part of it anyway, right Cory?"

Pooh turned to Cory.

"What's she talking about Cory? What does she mean by that?"

He was frozen solid, as was Arman' and I. We all were looking to Cory for an answer. I gripped AJ tightly as her finger seemed to get closer to squeezing the trigger.

God, don't let this crazy bitch kill us.

"So, Miss smarty pants, you wanna be his top bitch? Be his wife and live happily ever after? That's cool. There's only one problem with that... that's gonna be hard to do from the grave."

"Alicia, what the hell is wrong with you? Have you lost yo' damn mind," Pooh snapped.

"Yeah, Pooh I have. I lost it back when I lost my husband to this tramp and that damn baby. I could never compete with that bitch or that baby, right Arman', honey? Oh, I forgot, you can't remember... but I can!"

She aimed the gun straight at AJ and I freaked.

God, where are you? Don't desert me again.

Arman' leaned into my ear and told me not to panic, it would only make things worse.

"Look Alicia, although I can't remember what happened, it's pretty clear that I've hurt you. But why are you taking it out on my family? What have they done to hurt you? What has my son done to hurt you? He didn't ask to be here Alicia. Now if you want to kill me, fine. But why do you wanna hurt them? That won't undo any of this and it won't bring back the baby… our baby."

"She's not our baby," she screamed as she swung the gun over to Cory.

"It's ours, his and mines! And he let her die so no one would know about it."

Again, all heads turned to Cory. Arman' looked to him, waiting for his response. The silence was as thick as an ice berg until Arman' shook his head and told Cory to talk to him.

"C, man… tell me somethin'."

Cory stood still, still unable to say anything. That in itself was rare. Cory was always outspoken and determined to be heard. But today was different, for all of us.

Pooh's eyes began to water, reliving the drama of her ex-fiance' getting another woman pregnant on her but I'm sure that in no way could compare to this.

"Cory, say this ain't true."

No reponse.

"Say something dammitt!"

Cory gathered his temper and spoke calmly.

"Pooh baby, Arman', Moms, come on, now... I know ya'll know that wasn't my damn baby. She doin' this shit cause she's desperate now. Can't you see the bitch is crazy!"

"Liar!"

"Girl yo' crazy ass betta quit trippin' and put that damn thang down fo' yo' trick ass hurt somebody!"

"Fuck you, Cory!"

Pop, pop, pop, pop, pop...

It sounded as if she'd emptied the clip. We all hit the ground when she began firing. AJ started screaming and Arman had fallen backwards. I glanced over to see Momma J, lying still and praying out loud.

Pooh was hovering over Cory, who was bleeding profusely. When I looked up at Alicia, she was fumbling with the gun. I guess it had jammed on her.

It was a split second decision. I leaped up, left AJ on the ground and thankfully Arman' grabbed him into his arms. She saw me coming towards her and began fumbling with the gun even more. I don't know how much of my adrenaline was pumping but when I reached her, I drew back and punched her with eerything in me.

I hit her so hard in the face, she flew back inside the house onto the kitchen table and dropped the gun from her hand. She rushed me and we began to go at it, strong. I wrapped her hair around my fist and with my free hand, I began to pound against her face.

She was scratching at my face but I kept her at arms distance. She kicked me in my stomach and I fell back into the refrigerator. The pain shot down my neck to my back and down through my legs.

She reached inside the drawer and grabbed a knife. She came at me swinging wildly and I tried to run but she caught me on the arm. The blood spurted everywhere. She swung again and barely missed my face.

"You bitch! I'm so fuckin' sick of you! You stole my husband, my family… my life! I won't stop 'til I kill you!"

"You're gonna have to cause as long as I'm alive, it will always be me that he wants and I'm not giving him up Alicia, " I said, panting.

"UUUHHHH…"

She charged me again, this time landing the blade in my left shoulder. I fell to the floor with her on top of me. She was holding the knife above my head. My arms were getting to weak to fight her off any further. She grabbed my hair and Pooh came in landing a kick square across her face. She hit the floor and Pooh attacked.

"Bitch, you shot my man!"

Pooh punched and punched, landing them all up against her face and chest. Blood shot from her mouth across the hard tile floor.

Pooh grabbed her and began banging her head against the floor. Harder and harder she banged until Alicia's body went limp.

"Pooh, that's enough… enough baby," Momma J said, trying to calm her down and pry her hands from Alicia's hair.

"Come on now… stop dis here mess fo' you kill her."

Momma J dailed 911 and looked to me.

"You just hang in there baby… pray 'til theys get here."

Pooh ran over to me.

"Terri, you okay? Oh my God, you're bleeding pretty bad."

"I'll be fine, go and see about Cory. Go!"

She left and I began to black out. I couldn't hear anymore and my body went numb… but not before… I prayed.

ℭhapter Twenty Five...Arman'

".... And I wish never met her, met her at all..."

I had to help them. I placed AJ underneath the pinic table beside me.

"Stay here lil man, ok?"

He was holding on to me for dear life. He was screaming my name.

"Daaddyyy.... Daddy!"

"It's okay baby boy, daddy will be right back. No one's gonna hurt you."

I placed a kiss on his forehead. I could hear the sirens approaching in the distance. The moment was all too familiar. They were the last sounds I heard before I blacked out after the crash.

I looked over at Cory, gasping for air.

Damn.

My nigga was hurt pretty bad. Our lives together since the crash began to flash before my eyes. I needed to get to him.

I placed my hand under my left leg and brought it to my chest. Then I grabbed onto the chair beside me and began to pull myself up. Once I was standing, I began to wobble but I caught my balance rather quickly. I had a job to do and my family needed my help. I couldn't allow this physical handicap to keep me from handlin' my business. I took a small step before getting my equilibrium together. Then another and another... I was walking.

I made it over to Cory and plopped down beside him, exhausted.

"Hang in there man, help is comin'. I ain't gon' let you go out like this. We got too much to do, feel me? You had my back and now I definitely got yours. You my boy, can't nothin' come between that. You ain't never let me give up, I won't let you."

He looked to me, tears rolling down his face and blood seeping from the corners of his mouth.

"It wasn't like that man, I'm sorry... I..."

"Stop tryin' to talk man," I told him.

The tears flowing down my face as well.

"Save yo' strength. We got plenty of time to talk later. But right now, just hold on."

I glanced at his left ear and smiled at the tire shaped earring with gold spokes.

The paramedics came rushin' through the back gate and swarmed him. One of the officers helped me up and began to question me. I placed my hands up and told him to hold on, I had to go and get my son.

He saw me struggling to pull myself up and he rushed over to AJ and wrapped him in his arms. He brought him over to me and I held him tightly as he squirmed and cried for his mother.

Terri... where is she? Is she okay?

I needed to see her. I called moms over and instructed her and Ms. Carter to take AJ away from the area. Over to a neighbor's or something, anywhere but there. He didn't need to be traumatized any further by what was going on.

They began loading Cory into the ambulance and then procedeed to bring Terri out of the house on a stretcher. They stopped in front of me and I painfully glanced down at the woman I'd loved for what seemed like forever.

"Sir, we really need to move her. She's lost a lot of blood."

She was unconscious but I knew in my heart she could feel me there, just as I had been able to feel her. My heart ached to see her lying there like that. She had taken so much shit for me. Now she had risked her own life to save me and my family.

In that instant, I had made up my mind, that I would spend the rest of my life making this up to her, all of it. Everything she had taken for the sake of loving me or being with me, I would spend every breath making her feel it all was worth it.

Pooh finished up with the police and got into the car with a neighbor to follow Cory's ambulance. I couldn't believe she actually fell for him the way she did. She had his back and I admired that, especially after Kevin. They made a flossy couple though, I had to admit.

I glanced over and saw them bringing a handcuffed Alicia out of the back door. She was barely standing herself. I stopped them, waving them over to me. I held her face up to mine and looked deeply into her eyes. I was trying to find any lasting evidence of the woman I fell in love with once upon a time. I still saw traces of her, buried among all the hurt she had suffered. Some at my hands, most caused by life in general.

I still loved her and I really didn't want to see her this way. I couldn't help her but I loved her. She was crying hysterically.

"I'm sorry Arman', I'm so sorry... all I wanted was to have with you what she had with you. That's all I wanted."

I wrapped my arms around her and kissed her on the cheek.

"I know, I know. Alicia I'm so sorry I hurt you. I'm sorry you felt it had to come to this."

"Don't let them do this to me, please. Please... Arman'..."

They pulled her away from me and led her out the gate to an awaiting squad car. As I watched them drive away, I felt a tear roll down my face. I felt responsible for most of the situation.

My father Willie's words rung loudly in my ear.

"You's the big six dominoe son, when and how you's played determines the outcome of the game..."

She was a woman scorned by betrayal. Yet she'd gone to far over the edge for me to bring her back. I had to let her go... she needed help far beyond what I could offer her.

"Sir, we gotta hurry!"

He helped me over to the ambulance and the medics pulled me into the back with Terri.

"You're gonna be fine baby, I promise… just hang on," I told her, rubbing her hand as the small white medic placed an oxygen mask over her face.

I thought about Cory, fighting for his life inside the ambulance ahead of us. I then knew how he felt when he heard I had crashed that afternoon. The fear…

Nothing could ever make me stop loving him as my brother nor Alicia for that fact. They were apart of me. Yeah, there were issues that needed to be addressed but they would wait. Until then, we were still boyz. Down… like fo' flat tizes.

When we arrived at the hospital, they rushed Terri into surgery. I waited patiently for almost two hours, checking in constantly with Pooh concerning Cory and Momma J concerning my son.

After about four hours, they let me back to see Terri in recovery. I had to ask the nurse for a wheelchair because all the pressure I had put on my legs that day made them sore. I rolled into her room and parked beside her.

"Hey beautiful."

"Hey," she dryly answered. "Feels like de javu."

"Yeah, they say you're gon'be fine though. You've just gotta take it easy fo' while. Do a little physical therapy. I know this great lil room we can use."

She smiled and tried to laugh.

"You're so crazy. Where's AJ?"

"He's fine, He sleeping at Ms Patterson's house tonight cause Momma is cleaning up. So don't worry about him, worry about you."

I paused and stared at her.

"What were you thinking, running at her with a gun in her hand? She could've killed you."

She smiled.

"I was thinking about fighting. Fighting for my family... finally."

I returned her smile.

"Well from now on, that will be my job okay, not yours."

I picked up her hand and gently placed a kiss on it.

"I love you Terri. I loved you it seems from the first moment I laid eyes on you. The first touch, the first kiss. You're all I want and although I don't remember some things, I don't need to remember anymore to know that you are my soul mate. I never want to be without you and my son. Terri, say you'll marry me when all this is over."

The tears flowed down her face.

"But Arman', what about..."

"No buts... we've had enough conjuctions in our relationship. No more. I want you to be my wife. No if's, no and's and definitely no buts about it, What do you say?"

"In that case, I say yes. Yes Arman', I'll marry you."

I gripped the sides of the chair and stood to my feet. I leaned in and kissed her hard on the mouth. I gently bit her lips and nibbled my way around her face. God I'd missed that kiss. Even in darkness, I loved her; how could I not do anything else in the light? She'd be my life from that day forward and I'd never let anything nor anyone come between us again…

ℭhapter Twenty Six...Arman'

"... there's no pain that God is not able and willing to heal. All things work according to the Master's purpose and His Holy will..."

Three gun shots sent my nigga Cory to rehab and gave him a chance to overcome his new found addiction as well as deal with a lot of the issues of abandonment he had underlying his treatment towards women.

The military gave him nine months to get it together and be back in uniform. Since it wasn't a drug related shooting, he wasn't dishonorably discharged from duty. That was a good thing because Cory was always a hell of a soldier and could not easily be replaced.

Over the first few months, we went hard at it in physical therapy, both of us trying to get back into tip top shape. He'd spent countless hours explaining to me about the affair with Alicia and how he had envied me from childhood. My strength, my family bonds, my ability to both love and be loved.

He was able to express all that to me because he too had now found true love. It came in the form of Pooh. She'd stuck by his side through the entire ordeal and they had learned a lot from each other about trust and understanding. I was proud of him, I was proud of them both.

Alicia was sent to a Federal Mental Institution to begin serving her time in the Dallas/Forth Worth area. Convicted of Assault on government property (Cory), aggravated assault on Terri and weapon charges. It warrented her fifteen years behind the gate. Eleven and a half with good behavior.

I went to visit her at least once a month. Not because I felt sorry for her or still responsible for her condition but because she was too still apart of me and I still loved her. Love, real love has no boundries and it was that same real love that allowed Terri to understand my visits to Alicia. I would never turn my back on her nor pretend she didn't exist. How could I? Eleven years would eventually pass, then what?

Terri and I were married four months after my divorce was final with Alicia. We shared a double ring ceremony with Cory and Pooh. As I stood beside him, my brotha and my best friend, I watched the love of my life come towards me, finally.

Cory hit me on the arm.

"Aey dawg, ain't no mo' babies poppin' up is it?"

We laughed.

"Naw playa, no mo' drama fo' me."

He got quiet for a minute and then turned to me. He looked me in the eyes and I saw his eyes well up with tears.

"I love you nigga. You the best friend, the best brotha anyone could ever ask fo', you heard me?"

198

He reached in his pocket and pulled out a black box. De javu hit me all over again. It looked exactly like the one he pulled out in the dressing room before my last wedding.

I grabed the box and opened it. Inside was another matching earring to the one he was wearing. Exactly like the one I'd thrown out the window moments before I crashed.

"You must've lost yours in the crash so I got you another one made."

I hugged him tightly and we totally lost sight of the women walking down the aisle. We gripped each other in both forgiveness and love.

"You know we down…"

"Like fo' flat tizes," we said together.

As I grabbed Terri's hand and Cory took Pooh's, I glanced over to Moms and my son and smiled. I'd kept my promise to Willie after all. The one I had made before to him before he died. Never to let anything or anyone come between me and my shorty.

I never told anyone that at the sound of the Alicia's gun, my memory came flooding back. There was no need to. I had forgiven all and prayed to be forgiven. We had all been given a new chance at life. Even Alicia could now get the help she needed. And with that, I decided to let go…. Let go and let God!

199

Other Novels by Allysha Hamber

Keep It on the Down Low

Availble @ Barnes & Noble.com, Amazon.com and book stores everywhere.

The NorthSide Clit

Availble @ Barnes & Noble.com, Amazon.com and book stores everywhere

Unlovable Bitch

Coming Fall 2008

Mimika Avenue

Coming Summer 2009

Contact the Author:

www.myspace.com/diamondclit, lele4you@hotmail.com,

allysha4you@yahoo.com or

www.myspace.com/allyshahamber

Comments for Your Book Club:

Unlovable Bitch

What about me is so unlovable, that people simply
won't understand?
I've wracked my brain from front to back and thought
of everything that I can.
I've worn out my body for money, I've tried to gain
love by working my lips.
See a prospect in the vicinity and immediately add an
extra wiggle to my hips.
I've been beat down and abused, in everyway misused
but still, I keep on trying.
Always on my back, turning tricks for money stacks
but inside my soul is dying.
Been hit with a fist more times than I can count, my eyes
and my jaws stay swollen.
On the streets you mean nothin', you gain no one's respect,
when out there on the hoe strollin'.
But if you'll take a minute to peel back the layers of the
woman you see, beaten down by life,
You'll bare witness to the itch.
An itch, that only real love, in time can scratch
away but until then, I'm forever…
an **Unlovable Bitch***.*

Prelude…

What about me is so bad that people continuously want to hurt me? Why won't anybody love me?

Dream pondered this thought as she squeezed her eyes together tightly and winched at the intensity of the pain between her thighs. It was hot—so hot that Dream could have sworn that the tears falling from her eyes were made of pure steam.

Pieces, her pimp, was angry that Dream had lost his money for the second time that week to yet another trick.

The day had started off promising for Dream. Her goal was to turn enough tricks so that she could pay both Pieces his cut and still have enough money to rent a better room for her and her infant daughter. Maybe finally move into an affordable apartment of her own. Nevertheless, by the stroke of six o'clock, the day had quickly steamrolled downhill. Her last customer of the day made sure of that.

Silently, the tears rolled down her face as Frank's flesh, one of her once a month customers, beat down upon her used-up vagina. His heavy, two-hundred sixty-five pound body slammed down consistently against her frail, young frame. His breathing was labored, an indication that he had finally reached his quest. Dream's tears were symbolic of the emptiness, the pain and the shame she felt inside.

He was her eleventh trick of the day. Her vaginal lips were swollen and irritated from a long day's work. The muscles in her jaws were tired from the service six of them had demanded. Yet, Dream took comfort in knowing her baby girl had a roof over her head and her stomach was full from the pay.

Dream's body hurt like hell, her heart hurt…her soul hurt. What was the alternative? They had nowhere else to go. No family to take them in. For Dream, this was it, this was life...this was survival.

As the overweight customer, undoubtedly high on heroin, injected her with his disgrace, he rolled over, panting slowly and barked, "Go get me a glass of water!"

He exhaled strongly as Dream crawled from underneath the covers and headed for the bathroom. It felt as if someone had literally kicked her between her legs.

"That shol' is some good pussy you got there gal. If you ain't good for nothing else, you know you damn good fo' that."

Dream thought back to the first time she'd heard that from a man and frowned.

Fuck You! Dream spat out as she filled the dirty glass with water. She watched sadly as her tears began to mix with the swirling crystal liquid going down the rusty drain. She wished like hell she too could slide down into the tiny hole as well. As the two clear liquids blended, you could no longer tell where Dream's tears ended and the water began. As it was with every aspect of her life.

Where did the pain end? Where did peace and happiness begin?

"Let the water run some mo'. I want my shit real cold," he commanded.

While the water flowed from the faucet, Dream grabbed the soiled, dingy white washcloth from the towel rack and wet it underneath the coolness of the faucet water. She gingerly sat down on the crooked and cracked toilet seat, spread her legs apart and placed the rag onto her vagina lips as the tears continued to flow from her eyes. As Dream rested on the broken fixture, she continued to wet the cloth and apply it to the creases between her thighs to hold down the swelling.

In the distance, she heard the door to the hotel room close. She quickly reached over, turned off the squeaky faucet and exited the bathroom. She looked around the dimly lit room but there was no sign of her customer; he was gone. Her eyes quickly darted over to the dresser, searching for her sixty-dollar payment; thirty for the head she gave him and another thirty for the pussy she set out. It wasn't there.

She checked underneath the lamp and the pillows on the bed. All turned up empty. She looked over to the brown and orange sofa to see her blue secondhand purse, lying open.

Her heart sank and her stomach turned into knots as she picked up her coin purse from beside the rubble. Not only was her trick gone and had slipped out without paying her, but he had also stolen all of the money from her purse as well.

She angrily threw the coin purse down onto the floor and plopped down onto the soiled linen at the corner of the bed.

"Fuck! That's the second time this week! Pieces is gon' kill me! What the fuck am I gon' do now?"

Dream slowly rose from the bed and walked over to the dresser. She flicked a cockroach off her clothes, slid on her dingy beige bra and crusted beige panties. Despite the pain between her legs, Dream knew she'd have to go back out on the streets to make up Pieces' money, if not a dime more. He had let her slide once before when she'd come up short, with a promise she'd make it back up for him later in the week.

She put on her blue and white striped mini-skirt with its matching halter-top. It was her attention getter. She brushed her hair back into a banana clip and tried to fix up her face. Her eyes were swollen and dark red from crying. At seventeen, Dream's skin already showed signs of aging. She looked used up...she was used up and she was tired.

The room rent was due by twelve the next afternoon, which meant that Dream had a little less than twelve hours to recover Pieces' money and make enough for food, rent and diapers.

She walked over and knelt down beside the worn dresser drawer she had tried to make into a comfortable bed for her three-month-old daughter, Destiny. She was still sleeping soundly as she reached inside her diaper to make sure she was dry. She lifted the drawer onto the bed so the roaches were less likely to crawl on her, and then she grabbed her purse, shut the door behind her and went back out into the night.

The night had ended with Dream only making one hundred and eighty dollars. Three tricks were all she could handle because of the swelling of her vagina lips and walls. She knew she had to face Pieces and tell him what happened again, and she knew this time he probably wouldn't believe her.

So many times the girls on the streets used the story of being robbed by a customer as an excuse for not having his money. Usually it was because they were feeding a habit such as crack cocaine or boy and Dream knew Pieces would be fed up. She was right.

Pieces now towered above her, with her legs spread apart and her ankles bound to each corner of her old broken down, squeaky bed. Her hands were laced together by a dingy, twisted brown and white rope.

In Pieces eyes, he had been lenient with Dream once before and now he felt that she needed to be made an example of to the other young girls that he had out on the streets working for him.

In the pimping game, hoes took kindness for weakness and Pieces firmly believed that if you let them get over once, they would think it was okay to come at you with every bullshit excuse they could think of, as to why they didn't have his money.

Therefore, Pieces allowed no margin for error. The only reason he'd let Dream slip by without beating her the first time was she had made him a lot of money and he knew she had the unconditional grind inside of her back then.

However, once she experienced motherhood, in Pieces eye, her priorities became confused and getting him his money was no longer her main objective. So this time, he had to make a statement to her, just as he had done to Ebony.

Pieces had heated the tip of his nine-millimeter Beretta for the third time over the flame of the burning candle and inserted it into the bruised up vagina of Dream's battered body. Her left eye was swollen shut from his fist, and her right jaw experienced the same as her blood gushed from her mouth after she had served him on demand with her lips.

Dream looked over at the desolate creature crawling up the cracked, heavily stained wall of her rented room in the Jefferson Arms in downtown St. Louis. She envied the small creature at that very moment. Envied its ability to move when it wanted, go where it wanted and shield itself from danger as it wanted. She envied its freedom. It was something she had never known in her life before. True freedom was a luxury that she had never felt.

Growing up in the Darst Webb Projects of St. Louis, Dream was born to a mother who lived for the street life. At the age of thirty-three and the mother of three young girls, Dream's mother Karen, was a street whore in a different sense of the word.

Working as a Pharmacy Technician by day and a stripper by night, Karen rarely saw the inside of their home she shared with her three children. Dream and her sister's were often left to fend for themselves, knocking on their neighbors' doors in the project to ask for food, bathroom tissue and other necessities.

Dream was the youngest of the siblings and often found herself alone most of the time in the rough neighborhood. Her older sisters were often busy, running with their cliques, which left Dream vulnerable to the salt of the streets.

Dream's life changed dramatically after her father, Jerome died in a shootout in the Peabody Projects at the age of 34. He was the only person Dream felt safe around, and when Jerome died, Dream often felt she lost her life as well.

For Dream, Jerome's death was the beginning of a life full of both hell and misery. And as she screamed out in agony, the hot steel continuously blistering her now seventeen-year-old bloodied vagina, she reflected on the morning her life had changed from a life of promise, to a nightmare of despair...

Chapter One

Her virgin blood was everywhere. On the sheets, her pastel pink pajama gown and flowing freely from between her legs. Dream could barely move from the pain. The pain throbbed and pulsated throughout her body like she'd been beaten with a hammer. In some ways, she wished she'd had. Anything was better than the mental confusion and the emotional anguish she felt at that very moment.

His message was verbally clear, yet inside her nine-year-old mind, it had somehow been both entangled and crossed.

"Get up and go take a bath. Change that bed and clean up this room. And if anybody asks you why you changed them sheets, tell 'em you pissed in the bed. Shit, that ain't nothin' new. They'll believe it; you do it all the time."

He moved in closer to her and bent down to make his point clear. "Do you understand when I say you betta not say shit to nobody about this? 'Cause believe me, ain't nobody gon' believe you anyway. Hell, yo' momma don't even like you," he chuckled to himself.

"She tell me that shit all the time how she wish you was never born. And if you do tell anybody, she'll come ask me, and believe me, she'll take my side. Then she'll hate you even mo' fo' tryin' to break us up. Now hurry up, fo' them other lil' nosey bitches get home."

He stood up to fasten his wrinkled, dirty jeans and buckle up his belt. The look on his face no longer seemed affectionate to Dream. It was cold--dead almost--the same eyes she saw when her mother looked at her, un-loving and un-wanting.

Why would he say those things to me? I thought he loved me. That's what he told me when he brought me candy and toys. Just for me and not the others. When he bought me baby dolls and gave me a dollar for the bomb pop truck. Especially, when he said he wouldn't leave me, like my daddy did.

Ernest, Karen's drunken on-again off-again boyfriend, was a trucker who only breezed through town every other weekend. Since Karen was never home when he arrived, she gave him keys to their fifth-floor project apartment.

Ernest baited Dream into his web of isolation over the preceding months with candy, dollar bills and toys. He knew she felt unloved and deserted by her family and he used that greatly to his advantage. He gave Dream things when no one was around so she would idolize him and feel special.

As with any molester, from the first moment he entered the apartment with Karen, he'd set his sights on his mark. Dream was always off to herself and always seemed withdrawn from the group. Once he got in good, found out what type of woman and mother Karen really was, he knew he was in. He soon began to set his plan in motion.

It was Dream's birthday, a day her family either forgot about or didn't care about. That day was the day Ernest decided to make his move. He had brought Dream a Betsy Wetsy Doll, the one she had begged for every time she'd seen it on the TV and wanted for months.

When Dream saw the doll, her heart filled with excitement and appreciation. When she jumped into his arms, Ernest told her to kiss him. Like any other day, Dream placed a soft child-like peck on his left cheek.

Ernest sat her down atop his lap and plotted out his every move. "That's not a good kiss for a gift you've been wanting for so long, now is it?"

Dream hunched her shoulders and replied, "I don't know."

"Well, I'll tell you. No, it's not. I had to go all over the city to find you that doll. Not to mention I'm the only one who cared enough to get you a present. You see, yo' momma 'nem don't give a damn about you. I think you should try that kiss again and really show some thankfulness."

Dream repeated the kiss on his cheek, harder this time.

"Now Dream, that was a little better but not good enough. You love me don't you?"

Dream nodded her head in compliance.

"Well, here then. Let me show you how you suppose to kiss a man you say you love."

Ernest opened Dream's mouth and forced his tongue inside with such a force, Dream gagged and began to choke.

"You not doin' it right. Now if you want me to continue to bring you nice presents and shit, you've gotta learn this, understand?"

Dream's feelings were hurt that she wasn't pleasing the only person that seemed to care for her besides her Nana Grace. She wanted him to keep being nice to her and would do anything to please him. She didn't want him to leave her behind like her daddy did.

"You gotta relax."

Dream closed her eyes tightly and like she'd seen her older sisters do many times with their boyfriends, she opened her mouth to receive his kiss.

Ernest once again stuck his tongue inside her mouth. He leaned back and patted her on her back.

"Good, that was good, baby. Every time you see me from now on, that's how you kiss me—when no one is around of course. We don't want anyone to know about our special friendship, okay?"

Kisses turned to fondling, fondling to the jacking off of his penis, the jacking off of his penis to the splitting of the corners of her mouth as he shoved his over sized penis between her lips. That went on for months. Her splitting lips finally led to blood between her thighs.

Dream slowly climbed down off the dingy white twin sized bed and began cleaning the room she shared with her sister, Vanessa, her legs almost buckling from the pain. She picked up her panties, blue jean shorts and her yellow Big Bird T-shirt from the floor and placed them in the Hefty trash bag they used for a dirty clothes hamper.

The pinkish colored liquid continued to ooze down her legs. She went into the bathroom and ran herself a bath. She returned to the bedroom and began removing the soiled linen from the heavily urine-stained mattress.

At only nine-years-old, Dream was smart enough to know that if someone found the sheets in the laundry, they would question her about the stains. So she balled up the sheets and placed them inside the kitchen trash can and made a mental note to empty the bin once she got out of the tub.

Dream went into the bathroom and stepped into the tub. The usual temperature she liked her bath water was unbearable to her. Her vagina hurt like hell and she could see the water turning colors. She sat on the ledge of the tub, let out some of the water, and turned on the cold faucet to cool the water.

She went to replace the linen on her bed and returned to the tub. She was no longer crying outward, but inside she couldn't understand why Ernest was being so mean to her after she had given him what he wanted. The tears only began to fall as Dream thought back to what he'd said about her family and her mother, Karen's feelings towards her. She cried because she knew he was telling the truth. She had known it all along.

Karen would say things to her like, "Yo' damn daddy wasn't shit and you ain't gon' be shit just like him." Whether it was just wetting the bed or getting into trouble at school, Karen made sure she made her negative thoughts about her baby daughter known to her.

Dream sat in the water and soaked her swollen body parts as Ernest entered the bathroom with his keys in hand.

"Stop all that damn cryin'! Big girls don't cry. Now hush up and take it like a woman."

Dream dried her face and began to wash up as she heard the front door to the apartment close.

A big girl? Did you hear that? He said I'm a big girl! Doesn't he know I'm only nine-years-old?

Dream got out of the tub and began to put on her clothes when she realized that her vagina was still leaking. She went into the closet, grabbed a washcloth, folded it into fours and placed it down between her thighs. Then she gathered her remaining items and returned to her room before anyone came home. She then climbed onto her bed and grabbed the doll Ernest had just given her for a birthday present. She hugged the doll with all her might.

It didn't matter to her that the pain inside her body was unbearable, all that mattered in Dream's nine-year-old mind was the doll Ernest had given her. The gift from him represented a symbol of affection and love in her eyes. And no matter how twisted, it was something Dream wasn't used to feeling inside that home.

Chapter Two

Ernest didn't hear the keys jingling in the front door at one A.M., in time to finish the deed. Karen wasn't due home from the strip club until three.

Ernest had come into Dream's bedroom that night, smelling strongly of Jack Daniels as he had done once a week over the past six years. From a young girl, through puberty, to a young woman, Ernest had stripped away both Dream's childhood and her self-worth.

Inside, she felt the confusion of a young girl's mind trying to live in an adult-framed world. She wanted to be loved by him. She felt no one else neither cared about her nor understood her. She thought that as long as she did what he asked her to do to please him, he would always be there. She could never have been more wrong.

Karen could hear the soft squeaking sound of Dream's twin sized bed, along with a male's voice moaning as she rounded the corner towards her own bedroom. Her older two girls were away for the weekend, so she knew it was her youngest daughter probably having sex with some young boy from the block.

Karen had already begun suspecting that Dream was having sex because of the way her body was forming and developing. Her baby daughter's breasts sat up high at 38C's and her ass and thighs had surpassed Karen's by the age of twelve.

As Karen reached over and flicked on the light to Dream's room, she almost fainted. There was Ernest, pounding away on her fifteen-year-old daughter in the world famous doggy-style position.

When he heard Dream gasp and noticed the horrified expression on her face, Ernest turned to find Karen standing in the doorway with her hands covering her mouth. He immediately pushed Dream down to the mattress and leaped off the bed towards Karen.

Karen was frozen in time. Her heart quickly became enraged, but not towards Ernest, it was unleashed bitterly towards Dream.

"You triflin' lil' slut!" she screamed as she lunged towards Dream on the bed.

Dream scurried to the top of the mattress and quickly covered herself with the navy blue blanket.

Ernest wrestled to put on his clothes and begin trying to explain to Karen.

"Aey, baba...baby, it's not what you think! Wait! Calm down, let me explain."

Karen yanked Dream by the top of her head and dragged her out of the bed. Dream grabbed her mother's hands and tried to pry them a loose from her hair while kicking and screaming for her to stop and listen to her.

Karen unleashed a series of blows to Dreams face and head.

"I knew you were trouble! I knew yo' ass wasn't shit and I should've got rid of you a long fuckin' time ago. A wad of sperm I should've let hit the fuckin' wall!"

Ernest pulled Karen from on top of Dream and dragged her forcefully into Karen's bedroom.

When Dream heard the door slam, she scooted over to lock her bedroom door, put on some clothes and lay down on the floor to listen at the bottom of the door.

She knew Ernest would protect her. She knew he would straighten everything out with her mother. Yet, all she heard was

Ernest apologizing for having too much to drink at the Flamingo Lounge, and Dream coming into the living room with a T-shirt and no panties on. He lied and told Karen how Dream had flaunted her ass in front of him and bent down in front of the television as if she'd dropped something so he could see her pussy.

He even blamed Karen for always being gone when he came into town, and for working at the Pink Slip strip club over in East St. Louis.

Dream listened as he, the one person she thought loved her, manipulated her mother and turned her further against her daughter. He had simply added the match to the gasoline of hatred Karen had felt for her daughter for years.

Dream couldn't believe what she was hearing.

How could he say those things about me? It wasn't me who started this. All I did was try to please him. How can he say this shit about me? Why is he doing this to me?

Before Dream could reason within herself, Karen began to beat on her bedroom door, kicking it for Dream to open up and let her in. She wanted to hurt Dream for seducing the man she loved. She wanted to kill Dream as she reflected on both the joy and the pleasure in the sound of his voice, the sparkle she saw in his eyes once she hit the light switch and saw him fucking her.

Karen continued to punch the door with force. Dream withdrew to a corner opposite the end of the room, scared to death.

Finally it stopped, and Dream prayed it would all just go away but as she saw the knob on the door turn, she knew Karen had jimmied the lock with a knife.

Karen entered the room and stood in front of Dream with the blade in hand.

"Why? Why you do this? Who taught you to be such the little slut that you would stoop this low to fuck my man? I work two fucking jobs to keep a roof over yo' head, clothes on yo' back, food in yo' stomach and this is how you fuckin' repay me? You fuckin' nasty lil' bitch! You never wanted me to see me happy. Never wanted me to be around any man but yo' sorry ass daddy. Well get it through yo' fuckin' head, he dead! He ain't comin' back! He got his fuckin' head blown off, remember?"

That sparked off rage inside Dream as she lunged at Karen with fury. Karen swung the knife to stop Dream mid-stride and promised Dream she'd take her life her without hesitation or a second thought.

"I bought yo' nasty ass in this world, I guarantee, you lil' hoe, I'll take you out!"

"But Momma, how you gon' believe him? He lyin'!"

"What he gotta lie fo'? You always have been the problem child. Always getting' into shit, stealin' from the store, lyin' all the time and pissin' all over the place and shit. How the fuck you gon' fuck somebody's man and still pissin' all over the fuckin' place?"

"Momma, please! You gotta believe me! I didn't do what he said I did! This ain't the first time we done this!"

Karen swung around and looked to Ernest in the doorway.

"She's a fuckin' lie!" he screamed, pointing his finger at Dream.

"You said it yo'self, baby, she lies all the damn time. Nothin' but a trouble maker, always tryin' to ruin yo' happiness."

"Trouble maker? Tell her how you used to bring me candy and give me money to kiss you. How you use to tell me you loved me while you made me touch you in certain places. Tell her!"

"Now that's a fuckin' lie too, baby!"

Dream looked back to Karen and pleaded with her to believe her.

"It's the truth Momma. It's been going on since I was nine years old."

Karen backhanded Dream and she fell to the floor.

"Liar! Just shut up! Shut up!"

Dream grabbed her face as the tears flowed.

Why won't she believe me? Damn, does she really love him that much or does she really just hate me that much?

Everybody was turning on her, making her look like the bad guy. Karen, she was used to. Ernest...she couldn't believe!

She looked up to her mother and continued to plead with her.

"Momma, please, you gotta believe me. He's been having sex with me since I was nine years old!" Dream screamed out.

"Say it one more time Dream and I swear I'll..."

"Momma, it's the truth!"

"Get out! Get up and get yo' hoe-ish ass out of my house, now!"

"*What?*" Dream whispered.

"Get out!"

"Momma, please don't..."

"I said, get the fuck out, Dream!"

Karen grabbed Dream by the arm and began to drag her out of the bedroom. Dream grabbed Karen's leg with her free arm and begged Karen to listen to her.

Karen released her arm and reached down to grab both of Dream's legs and continued to drag her through the hallway, belly up.

Dreams eyes pleaded with Ernest to help her as he stood off to the side with a slight smirk on his face.

"Please, Ernest! Please help me! Please tell her! Why are you doing this to me? You said you loved me, please, help me…"

Karen unlocked the front door, snatched Dream by her shirt and pushed out the door. She locked the door behind her as Dream stood on the outside, screaming and banging to get in.

Karen walked over to outstretched arms of Ernest and cried. Inside, she wanted to believe Dream was a liar. She couldn't bear to think, let alone except the reality of Dream's story. Couldn't imagine that type of horrible act going on all those years in her very own home underneath her very own nose. Therefore, the easiest thing to do was to block it all out, and the best way to do that was to get rid of the one thing that would always remind her of it; her daughter.

Chapter Three

Dream resigned from the door once it had become clear that Karen was not about to let her come back inside the apartment. She walked down the dirty, graffiti sprayed hallway to the elevator. The overwhelmingly strong odor of urine almost burned her nostrils as she waited for the elevator to reach the ground level.

Dream clutched her chest as she walked by all the local people still hanging out on the courtyard. She had almost made it across the parking lot of her Auntie's neighboring Peabody Projects parking lot when she saw them; crowd of young bucks, hanging out and shooting dice.

None of their faces looked familiar to her and Dream was afraid to walk by them. She sped up her pace but not fast enough to get by them unnoticed.

One of the young bangers called out to her as she passed them by. "Hey, Ma, what you doing out here this time of night? What you looking fo'? I got that heat fo' ya."

Dream responded by picking up her pace even faster and the young bangers responded by following her. As she heard the footsteps behind her get closer, She started running in fear for her life and kept running until she could run no more. One of the young bangers caught her by the shirt and yanked her down to the ground. One of his crewmembers grabbed both of Dreams legs and together they carried Dream behind a dumpster. She kicked and kicked at them as they tried to pry her legs apart but her efforts were to no avail.

It was a four-man conspiracy of rape, sexual battery and humiliation. As one took down her panties, one held her arms down on to the dirty ground mixed with mud, drug needles, broken glass and trash. The third forced Dream's head towards his body and told her to open her mouth. When she didn't comply, he punched Dream in her left jaw and continued to punish her until she obeyed.

The older one was already inside her, tearing away at her flesh, while this one was getting his satisfaction from her orally. The fourth culprit stood lookout as he patiently awaited his turn. Dream could hardly breathe, her jaw hurt like hell from his blows and the force at which he continuously shoved his penis in her mouth, made the pain that much more intense.

It seemed as though simultaneously, they unloaded their filth onto her body, the first inside her ailing vagina, the second disgracing her with his fluids all over her face. As his sperm mixed with Dream's tears, she silently wished they would just kill her, end the misery she had felt within her soul for so long.

After the other two took their prospective turns, Dream was left behind the dumpster, hunched over in pain and still bleeding from the inside of her now severely swollen jaw. She was lightheaded as she tried to stand to her feet. Her clothing was torn from top to bottom.

She stumbled across the dirt-filled pavement towards 9th Street. All that was covering her bare chest were her arms, and her ripped up shorts were barely hiding her bottom.

When she reached the main street, she walked as fast as she could, given the pain, to try to reach the Mobile gas station a few blocks ahead. She was tired, more so emotionally than physically.

Just as she thought she could go no further, a black Monte Carlo pulled up beside her. At that moment, Dream was feeling so much disparity she didn't care if he wanted to go at her for round two. She wouldn't have even tried to fight back.

However, as the car came to a slow halt and the passenger side window descended, a middle-aged woman called out to her.

"Are you alright? Say, do you need some help?"

Dream ignored the woman and continued to stumble down the block. She was almost there but her legs alone could go no further. She stopped to address the woman in the driver's seat.

When Dream turned towards her and the woman saw the shadow of her face, she threw the car in park, jumped out and ran towards Dream. When she saw her up close, she wrapped her arms around her and allowed Dream to place her weight against her body.

"Who did this to you?" the woman asked.

"It doesn't matter," Dream whispered quietly.

"It does matter! Did your boyfriend do this to you?"

Dream didn't respond.

Boyfriend? Lady, you just don't know! You really don't wanna know. You wouldn't believe me if I told you anyway.

The woman escorted Dream to her car and formally introduced herself.

"My name is Kim. What's your name?

"Dream."

"Dream? What a beautiful name."

Beautiful? Lady, you really trippin'. Nothin' about me is beautiful.

"Well Dream, do you think you can let me take you the hospital and get you looked at? You really need to see a doctor."

The woman opened her passenger side door and helped Dream inside. She went back to the trunk of the car to remove a sports jacket from inside. She gave Dream the jacket to cover herself, laced the seat belt around Dream's waist and closed the door. She walked around to the driver's side and entered the car.

"Well Dream, whoever did this to you, you didn't deserve it no matter how you feel right now or what anybody says. I'm so sorry this happened to you. Is there anyone I can call for you?"

Dream didn't even have to bust her brain on that one. No, there was no one she could call for her. No one who cared about her or her welfare, especially Karen.

If she did, she wouldn't have put me out the house at two a.m. in the first damn place.

Kim took Dream to Cardinal Glennon Children's Hospital on Grand Avenue. When they entered the Emergency Room, Kim walked Dream to the counter and asked for help.

As Dream sat in the examination room with her legs up in stirrups, she stared off at the ceiling. She was wishing her Nana were still alive.

She would help me, I know she would.

She bit down on her bottom lip as the doctor inserted the steel metal clamp into her bruised vagina and cried.

"Call the police and Social Services now! This child has been savagely raped. There's massive tearing to the tissue," the doctor told the older female nurse.
"Who did this to you, young lady? Did you get a good look at them?"

When Dream didn't respond, the doctor finished her exam and walked to Dream's bedside.

"Sweetheart, I know you're scared. You have every right to be. But we are here to help and we can't help you if you won't let us."

The only thing Dream could think about were the words Ernest had spoken to her: *"...And you betta not tell nobody. They won't believe you anyway. If you do, I'll never love you again..."*

Dream couldn't understand why that still mattered to her but in a strange way, it did. She couldn't stand the thought of going back to the days when absolutely no one loved her.

The elderly black doctor patted her on the thigh.

"It's okay. You don't have to tell me. We've called your mother, she's on the way."

Dream's heart lightened at the thought of Karen being worried about her and coming to get her. In Dream's mind, that must have meant that Karen had forgiven her but what Dream would soon find out was that "coming" sometimes, meant "going".

When Karen entered the room, Dream was asleep. Karen browsed over the room, the walls and everything else except her daughter. She didn't want to look at her; she couldn't look at her. Karen despised her for the turmoil she felt inside. She sat in the chair next to Dream's bed and waited for the doctor to come inside to speak with her.

"Mrs. Wilson, hello, I'm Dr. Carter. I was the attending physician when your daughter was brought in."

"Who bought her here?"

"A concerned woman was passing by on her way home from work. She saw her walking the streets in this condition and quickly brought her here to the ER. I'm sorry to have to tell you this but she's been brutally raped."

"Ump, so *you* say! I bet you any amount of money it didn't go down like that."

"Excuse me? Ms. Wilson, never in the years of my medical experience have I seen a young woman's vaginal tissue that torn and bruised from having consensual sex with someone."

"Look doctor, you don't know my child like I do," Karen said, raising her voice.

The elevation in her vocal cords caused Dream to awaken. The doctor, disgusted with Karen, rubbed Dream's lower calf.

"Well, I'm gonna leave you two alone to talk. And Dream, please think about what I said."

When the doctor left the room, Karen once again did her best to let the distaste she felt for her daughter known.

"Look at you! You just simply live for make my life hell don't you? Got me all up in this fuckin' hospital with these people looking at me like I'm crazy and shit. Look at yo' clothes, look how yo' fuckin' draws look! You are so fuckin' nasty... you... you just embarrassin', that's all."

Dream felt the tears fall once again. She had hoped that finally Karen was there to comfort her and take her home. But as she watched Karen walk to the door, purse in hand, she learned the hard way, she wasn't.

"Did you tell them why you was out there in the damn streets this time a night in the first damn place? I bet you didn't tell them how I caught yo' lil' nasty having sex with a grown ass man less than two fuckin' hours ago, did you?"

Karen waved her hand in the air.

"Well, guess what? I ain't finna be in and out no fuckin' court with these white people all in up my business. You wanna be a hoe, be a hoe, but you won't be one under my damn roof! Let them take care of yo' ass from now on."

With that, she walked out and Dream felt the world settled down upon her shoulders. She picked up the remote from the stand next to her and turned on the TV. Since it was a children's hospital, the programming went off at eleven p.m. and so the only thing Dream could do was listen to the radio. Out came a song that told the story of her soul. The feelings that Dream as a child could not say nor understand. But as she lay there all alone, the music became a lullaby to her pain.

"*...She faced the hardest times, you could imagine and many times, her eyes fought back the tears. And when her youthful world was about to fall in, each time her slender shoulder bore the weight of all her fears. And a sorrow no one hears, still rings in midnight silence, in her ears...*"

Dream couldn't imagine someone else in the world knowing how she felt at that moment, but the song spoke to her heart.

"*...Let her cry for she's a lady. Let her dream, for she is a child. Let the rain fall down upon her. She's a free and gentle flower, growing wild...*"

Dream understood the words perfectly. And the fact that her name flowed freely in the song connected even more to her spirit. She didn't think she could hurt that intensely but she did. She grabbed the pillow and continued to cry. She cried and cried until she cried her soul out, only she didn't even think anyone, even God cared enough to listen.

UNLOVEABLE BITCH

FALL 2008

LaVergne, TN USA
10 January 2011
211849LV00004B/20/P